ANDREW

HOLLISTER - BOOK ONE

KRIS MICHAELS

WWW.KRISMICHAELSAUTHOR.COM

FOREWORD

Dear Reader,

This story deals with the difficult topic of suicide. Although the actual act is not depicted in the book, it is discussed by the characters.

CHAPTER 1

A ndrew Hollister forced his eyes open. White dust floated around him, the granular flakes fluttering on the breeze like the snowstorms of his childhood. A sensation of sound reverberated through his body, penetrating the haze that surrounded him. The deep thrum echoing around him quieted and took a giant step back. Replacing it, a sharp squeal assaulted his ears. A bloodied face appeared over him. His mind skipped back online, and pain shot through his body. "Jose." The sight of his gunnery sergeant acted like an electric shock, jolting him back to the here and now.

"Get your ass up, Cap!" His M4 was thrust into his hands as the garbled words registered. He grabbed the gun, his thumb automatically ensuring the firing selector was on automatic. He glanced down, gathering himself enough to pull the magazine, check the load, and slip it back into the weapon. The oily slime on his hands made the action difficult. He wiped the film onto his desert camouflage flak vest, *only then noticing it was blood that covered his hands. He gasped as pain crushed against him. His body howled in protest when he rolled to his side. His right leg wouldn't cooperate and his lower gut burned, on fire with the heat of a hundred suns, but he pushed up behind the remnants of a small plaster wall.*

"Status!" Andrew grabbed at Gunny Sanchez, his blood-soaked hand finding a hold on the

gunny's Kevlar vest. Andrew pulled him back so he could read the man's lips because his hearing was still fucked.

"Pip is down. FNG is out. On your left!" Gunny lifted his weapon and opened fire.

Andrew swiveled, identified his target, and pulled the trigger, taking down the man he targeted.

"Where are the rest?" He screamed the words as he fired.

"Dead." Gunny's single word encapsulated the frenzy around him. Frisco, Toker, Fish, and Razor—gone. Jesus. He leaned into his M4 and raged against the onslaught of the enemy.

Genevieve Wheeler glanced at the vibrating phone that skittered across the stainless steel countertop and grimaced. Not so much because of the caller but, as usual, the timing of the call sucked. Even after all this time, her mother seemed to have the innate ability to call at the absolute worst times. If she were true to form, and she would be, her mother would undoubtedly call back until she picked up. Gen sighed, slapped her hands together to rid them of excess flour, and grabbed for the phone. Pinning the phone between her cheek and shoulder while reaching for another pan, she answered, "Hello."

"I am surprised you answered and didn't let it go to voicemail... again." The deep Southern accent on the other end of the line flooded the airwaves, attempting to make her feel guilty, but Gen had become immune.

"I've been busy, Mom. Sorry," she apologized but had to add, "Remember the business I own? To succeed, you have to invest time and effort." She wiped off one hand and put the phone on speaker, dropping it beside her workstation.

"It's hardly a business, dear. You have a small diner in the middle of absolutely nowhere, *and* you only serve a limited breakfast menu."

"And lunch," Gen added. She was damn proud of her business.

"And lunch. Tell me, in a town of three hundred and fifty people, how do you expect to make a go of it? You do realize your father and I won't bail you out when you figure out you've wasted your entire inheritance from Grandmother Wheeler. Honestly, I don't see why you couldn't stay here and open a proper dining establishment."

Gen worked while her mother talked, carefully loading twelve sheet trays of caramel and cinnamon rolls into the industrial-size proofer while she halfway listened to her mother's usual rant. Gen looked toward the ceiling and took a deep breath. "How long have you been saying I'll fail? I haven't."

"But you aren't succeeding, either. You make enough to get by."

"Mom, I make more than enough and I'm happy. That is what matters, not money." She'd learned that life lesson from her grandmother, thankfully.

"Speaking of being happy, you'd be married with a family by now if you'd stayed in Birmingham."

Gen rolled her eyes. How many times did she need to have this conversation with her mother before the woman would let it rest? "You know the reasons I didn't stay, Mom. I'm happy here." She wiped her hands on her apron and leaned against the long, stainless steel worktop that ran down the center of her small diner's kitchen. "And, as a point of clarification, you know I would never ask you to pay for my mistakes. Dad didn't raise me that way."

Her mom let that little snipe go and redirected the conversation. "Avery called again last night." *Wow, okay... that was an unpleasant blast from the past.* Gen sucked a breath, trying to prevent the cuss words bouncing on the tip of her tongue from spilling out of her mouth. Her mother hurried on, preventing Genevieve from worrying about her language. "Really, he is *so* remorseful, he knows he made a mistake, honey, and it's not like you to be so unforgiving."

Stunned, Gen barked out a harsh laugh. "Mom, he

was engaged to me and having an affair with my best friend. I caught them together. For God's sake, they were having sex in my bed, and he's remorseful? Really, don't you think he *should* be? But you know what I find hysterical? It took years for him to come to that conclusion." The audacity of the asshole.

Gen's mom interrupted, "Well, of course, he should be, and he is, terribly so. You know he is grieving. He's miserable."

"Wait, what? Grieving what?"

"Well, losing you, of course," her mother purred.

Gen busted out, laughing, "Ah, hello? He's been married and divorced and he's grieving something he messed up years ago? Mom, I really think you're being sucked into his psychosis. I dodged a huge bullet when I caught him with Chelsea. That man is a serial cheater." At least, according to Chelsea's social media posts. The woman was all about airing their dirty divorce laundry in public, which probably pissed off the mighty Montague family.

"Don't buy into everything you read online, dear. Chelsea was bitter."

Gen nodded and rolled her eyes even though her mom couldn't see her. "I have firsthand knowledge of that feeling. It sucks, but she'll get over it. I did. Can I suggest you stop talking to him? He's ancient history, and frankly, he's a weasel."

"Honey, men will be men… they *all* make mistakes. Won't you please talk to him? I could give him your number. He really is a good man, so very successful and handsome. Gen, honey, he realizes he has made a mistake."

Gen pinched the bridge of her nose and answered, slowly enunciating each word very carefully.

"Mother, don't give Avery my phone number, my address, or the location of my diner. There is nothing left to talk about. I don't need an apology. I don't want one. He needs to move on because believe me... *I have.*" Years ago. Why the hell was this coming back around? *What's dearest Mom up to this time?*

A long pause at the other end of the phone caused Gen to look at the device to make sure she still had a cell connection. "Hello?"

"Gen, honey, I gave him your address last night. He said he only wanted to write you a letter to explain. It is just a post office box number. What harm could come from that?"

Genevieve shook her head, astonished at both Avery and her mother. "Mom, you said it yourself. This is a town of three hundred fifty people. If he wanted to find me, it wouldn't be hard." Not that he would. The man couldn't be an hour's drive away from his tanning salon. Gen rolled her eyes again. A question popped into her head. "Mom, tell me something. Why now? What's happening to make him think of me? There's something else, isn't there?"

"Honey, he just wanted to write a letter and asked for your address last night at your father's political fundraiser." Her mom added quickly, "We have the full backing of the party. Your father is going to make a run for President."

"In two years?" Gen frowned at the phone and wiped her workspace.

"No, six. The incumbent will be the party's nomination. But we are building his platform now and slotting in public appearances. There is so much to do. As you know, image is everything, so mending the fences with Avery, especially due to his father's political position… Well, it needs to happen."

"What? Does Dad know about this?" Gobsmacked, she stopped cleaning the counter.

"Of course. Reporters dig, darling."

"Right. So, how are you going to explain the separation between you and Dad and the fact Dad raised us without you?" She could only imagine her mother's scheming and manipulation at a national level. *God help us all.*

"That's something we're working on. Our issues we can take care of, you need to fix yours."

Gen snorted. "I don't have any issues, Mom."

"Good, then you won't mind talking to Avery. His parents insisted he contact you, and I agree. Showing a strong joint front will not only help your father but Avery's father. Oh, pooh, I forgot I have a nail appointment. I must go. Toodles."

Gen stared at the phone and shook her head. "Seriously?" she spoke to the phone. "The only issue I have is you."

"Who?" Eden Wheeler, her sister-in-law, asked from the back door.

Gen spun and grabbed her chest. "Holy hell, woman. Knock next time."

Eden laughed and shifted Carmen, Gen's niece, in her arms. Gen slapped off the remnants of flour from her hands and reached out. "Give me that adorable baby girl."

She took the baby and fell into a swinging step across the floor.

"Do you need any help, and who do you have issues with?" Eden walked over to the walk-in refrigerator and pulled out two water bottles, setting one down for Gen and taking a long drink out of the other.

"No, I'm done except for a bit of cleanup. And Mom is my issue, as always. Why are you in town? And I'm so sorry that movie night didn't go as anticipated." Eden had to come into town to get the kids because of the situation at the Marshall Ranch, which had caused Gen to open and feed thirty hungry men in the middle of the night.

Gen pulled her ponytail out of Carmen's little hands and flipped it over her shoulder. "Aunt Gen doesn't want to go bald. No, she doesn't." She rocked Carmen again and gave the little girl her finger to hold to divert her niece's attention from her hair.

"Well, as you know, Jeremiah was gone all night,

too. I was happy to come get them. That ranch house is too quiet without anyone there. Zeke called me before the sun came up this morning and asked if I could help him. I just got back from the Marshall Ranch and picked up Carmen. Jay is out back playing. They stayed with Sarah Granger. She didn't mind helping out."

Gen sighed. She wouldn't mind watching them either, but she'd had zero sleep last night after she handed off the children to Eden and she was running off massive quantities of coffee and willpower today. "I don't know what was going on out there last night and this morning, but something big happened." She glanced at her sister-in-law, hoping for a nugget of information.

"Sorry, signed my life away. Can't say a word about anything. Suffice to say that it's over."

Gen held Carmen and started to wipe down the counter one-handed. Eden stepped in and took over, wiping the counters down like a pro. Gen shifted Carmen and bounced her a bit, settling her. "Do they have everything they need? Is there any way I can help?"

"They have everything under control. I know they'll ask if they need assistance, but I think they're good to go," Eden explained.

Well, that made sense. Everyone helped around here. It was what they did. A culture she'd learned to love. Gen spun. "Oh, I met Ember King last night, or this morning, rather. She's nice. And so pretty. She's Amanda Marshall's daughter-in-law."

"Ember? Yes, she is nice. I've met her a couple times. Remi knew her when they were in residency together. She lives in Nevada or somewhere down there with her husband." Eden rinsed out the cleaning cloth in the sink.

"I'm glad she was here last night. It was busy and she pitched in along with Remi. We emptied the walk-in fridge feeding the lot that showed up. I'm going to have to make a run to Rapid City sooner than planned to restock." There had been a fat check placed onto her counter sometime during the day with a note of thanks. She wasn't expecting to be reimbursed, especially ten-fold the amount she'd provided, but with that check, she could close for a day during the week to make the run.

"What did the Women's Circle have to say about last night? They did come in for all the gossip, right?" Eden glanced at her.

Gen rolled her eyes and groaned. "Coffee, cinnamon rolls, and gossip. Like clockwork. I swear, they are the busiest busybodies in the world. They had zero information, and nobody in the diner knew anything, or if they did, they weren't giving them anything. I think Edna Michaelson actually went over to Jeremiah's clinic to try to get some gossip because she'd seen several of the men going in and out of the building this morning," Gen laughed, "but the front door was locked, and a particularly abrasive gentleman refused to allow her in the back door." Gen mimicked Edna's snooty tone. "Father Murphy had stopped in for a coffee about that time and took her to task for snooping. I had to come into the kitchen to keep from laughing in front of her."

"I swear, she's getting bolder as she gets older. I say good on Father Murphy." Eden wiped her hands and held them out.

"Thanks for the baby fix." She leaned down and kissed her niece before she gave her back to her mom.

"Can I get a takeout for dinner tonight? I didn't defrost anything before I left this morning." Eden bounced Carmen on her hip.

"Sure. What do you want?" She opened the walk-in freezer. "I'm fully stocked."

"Gumbo, please, and some of your garlic bread. Jay and Remi requested it, special."

"You got it." She pulled out the containers and dropped them into a bag.

"Gen, have you ever thought of hiring help?"

She looked up from stuffing napkins and hot sauce packets into the bag. "More than once, but who am I going to hire? Edna? No, thanks."

Eden's eyes widened. "Goodness, that would be a horrid mistake."

"Right? Besides, I have all of this down to a science. The biscuit ingredients are measured out and ready to be mixed with the wet ingredients in the morning.

Sausage and ham slices are prepped and ready for the oven, and everything is set for my morning customers. Lunch starts at the lull about nine, and I clean up and prep before I go up about five. Easy peasy."

"I don't know how you do it. Thirteen-hour days, six days a week." Eden grabbed the bag.

"Willpower, but I shut down early on Saturdays most times." She laughed, kissed Carmen, and opened the door for Eden. She watched them walk toward the front of the building before she shut the door. The utter exhaustion from what had turned out to be a twenty-four-hour day the day before coupled with the weirdness of her mom's call hit like a tidal wave. She took another look around her small kitchen. She'd upgraded the equipment and improved the front of the house after a tornado nearly wiped out the town. Her fingerprint was on every square inch of the place, and she loved it. With a sigh of utter contentment, she turned off the lights and headed upstairs for the night.

The alarm shrilled at four in the morning. Rolling over to slap it, Gen blinked the sleep from her eyes. The sky was still dark but would lighten quickly. This morning, waking up took a substantial effort, probably because of the sleepless stint the night before. Normally, she was up before the alarm. She yawned and closed her eyes, her body floating on the comfort of her mattress.

Maybe she needed to take steps toward getting help at the diner. Jerking herself awake, she flipped back the blanket and headed to the bathroom. After a quick shower, she pulled her hair back into a ponytail and donned her work clothes. Her uniform was the same every day: blue jeans, a T-shirt sporting the words 'Gen's Diner' on the back, and damn good tennis shoes with bouncy heels and arch support. She was on her feet all day every day and needed the comfortable attire.

The walk down the stairs from her apartment to her diner took no time. She opened the back door and flipped on the light switch, illuminating the kitchen. Within minutes, Gen became lost in the familiar routine of making two huge, fifty-cup urns of coffee, putting the caramel and cinnamon rolls into the oven, and mixing up the waiting biscuit dough. When the yeast rolls were done, she put four sheet pans of biscuits into the convection oven and started the sausage and ham cooking in the regular industrial-size oven on the other side of the kitchen. Most of her early morning crowd would be sitting down by five-thirty, which gave her thirty minutes to drink more coffee and try to wake up.

She took a cup of coffee to the front window and drank it as she peered out at the sleepy little town. It was her routine. Every morning, she stood here and took stock of the wonderful town she'd been fortunate enough to find. Across the street and down about a block was her brother Jeremiah's medical building. His psychiatry practice seemed to do well. She never asked about his patients. It wouldn't be right. Zeke, the town doctor, worked in the same building, as did Eden when Zeke needed a hand or someone to cover during an emergency. Like yesterday. She shook her head. Whatever had happened at the Marshall Ranch was being held tight against the vest, which was normal. Something to do with the Guardian people who worked out at the ranch, she assumed. They were salt-of-the-earth people who fit into this small community seamlessly. She hoped everything had been patched up no matter what had happened.

Phil Granger's filling station had a light left on in the bay all night. She'd hear him grumble about that today when he came in for coffee. Phil could pinch a penny hard enough to make it squeal like a stuck pig, but the man would give you the shirt off his back. His wife, Sarah, was cut from the same cloth. Gen rented her garden space from Phil. He was one of the few that owned land in Hollister. Most rented the land they had their businesses on from the Hollisters. Senior didn't want to sell the land, but he made it easy for people to settle in the area. The man was as bristly as a pissed-off porcupine, but he had to have a soft spot somewhere because he was damn good to the town.

She sipped her coffee and glanced down the little main street. Hollister didn't have much to draw or keep a person. Sanderson's Market, the hardware store, two churches—on opposite ends of the road—a barber-slash-beauty shop that was open when the owners had customers, Phil's garage and fuel pumps, Jeremiah's medical building, and her small diner. The stockyards were outside of town. Declan's bar, The Bit and Spur, was close enough to walk to but still just outside of what people called the town. The little county office that was open two days a week was located next to the two-story school. Kindergarten through high school were taught in the same building, and the children were bussed in from all the ranches. This year's graduating class had ten students. She chuckled to herself. There were over seven hundred in her graduating class in Birmingham. Twice the population of this hamlet.

She glanced at her watch and stirred herself out of her musings. Flipping on the lights, she unlocked the front door and changed her 'Closed' sign to 'Open.' She headed back to the kitchen and fell into the routine of opening for the day. Gen topped the cooled cinnamon rolls with a thick cream cheese frosting in between life-sustaining gulps of coffee. She buttered the tops of the hot biscuits and put them on a rack, allowing them to cool enough to handle.

The bell that sat above the door jingled. She walked out to the front and smiled at Doc Macy, the local vet. Based on the condition of his clothes and the mud on his boots, he had obviously been up all night, working

"Sorry, Genny, I tried to stomp them off on the sidewalk, but I still think I am going to track." His open and warm smile echoed his genuine, caring personality.

"It's all good, Doc, that's why I have brooms and mops. Did you pull another all-nighter?" Gen pulled a coffee cup out and filled it for him.

He nodded and ran his hands through his thick blonde hair. His neatly trimmed beard softened the sharp, masculine angles of his handsome face, and the dark circles under his hazel-blue eyes gave him a haggard look. His forty-something face showed hints of an older man this morning. "Yeah, a tight calving season tends to lend itself to sleeplessness. I don't anticipate a full night's sleep for the next forty to sixty days." Doc Macy nodded toward the kitchen. "Sausage biscuits ready yet?"

Gen nodded. "Coming right up. Are the ranchers having problems with calving?" She walked behind the counter and assembled his breakfast.

"Just the normal stuff. Hollister had three cows go down damn near simultaneously. Andrew turned and pulled one while I worked another. Ryan tried to turn one, but the cow's uterus ruptured. We saved the little guy but had to put the mom down. Ryan should be coming in with her for the meat processing plant. Damn shame, too, that was a good cow, and she produced some mighty fine little ones."

"Such a shame," Gen agreed as she left Doc Macy to his food. She knew the Hollisters could absorb the loss, but around here, cattle built livelihoods, and the ranchers took damn good care of them.

The early morning clientele trickled in. Genny lost herself in the routine and conversation. She sold out of cinnamon rolls again today, the third time this week she'd run out. She mentally calculated the recipe to increase the amount she baked to up the yield to seven sheet pans. The ranchers and stockyard workers left as she made another urn of coffee for the second wave of customers. School teachers on the way to work stopped by for takeout coffee and rolls or biscuits, the clerks at the hardware store would send someone down after they opened for the day, and Phillip Granger would wander across the street and eat a roll and drink some coffee when it was slow at the gas station. Several ladies came in routinely and read their newspapers, books, or e-readers while drinking coffee and watching the people in town. Office workers at the new county building stopped in often for food and conversation when they were working. For a small town, the population the diner served was more than respectable.

Gen watched one of her friends, Allison Sanderson, walk across the street. She worked at her family's market. The store had essentials and a few other odds and ends that the Sandersons stocked for regulars, plus Allison and her mother baked and sold the best sour-dough bread. Allison was an opinionated, sharp-tongued personality with fiery red hair and a bossy attitude. She was fun and a handful.

Gen poured Allison a cup of coffee in a to-go cup.

"Busy this morning?" Allison's large, blue eyes scanned the diner.

Gen shrugged, "No more than usual. Steady stream of customers."

Allison lifted her eyebrows, "So, why the black circles and lack of your famous bubbly Alabaman personality?"

Gen cast a glance around. "Mom called yesterday afternoon. She's scheming again. I just don't know what it is. I need to talk to Jeremiah or call my dad. The conversation was weird with a capital W."

"Ugh... what could she be up to this time?" Allison held up a hand. "Wait, let me guess. She's going to send the Alabama faction of the Deadbeat Debutante Hunters up here and force you into a revival in which you will renounce the heathen ways you are now living and miraculously return to her as a pristine princess that she can manipulate into her 'Mini-me!'"

Gen choked on a gulp of coffee she'd taken, and they both laughed. "Girl, don't even think of such things! If that woman thought for a minute a scenario like that would work, I'd be abducted tomorrow."

"Well, I'm sure as hell not telling anyone, and if you turn up missing, I've already promised to point a finger toward your mom."

"See, this is why friends are so important," Gen

laughed, and Allison picked up the coffee along with three small creamers and a packet of sugar substitute.

"Thanks for the joe. Oh, Dad wanted me to ask if there was any chance you were going to Rapid anytime soon."

"Yeah, the other night cleaned me out of a few things. I'll go one day this week. I'm going to close so I can leave early. Got a list?"

"Yep. I'll get it together and bring it over later. Don't forget to put a note up on the door or people will be here wanting breakfast. Later." Allison ambled out of the café as three men entered. Gen recognized two but the third one she hadn't seen before. He seemed to dwarf the diner and everyone in it. She acknowledged the men as they entered.

"Hey, Ryan, good to see you." The cowboy dipped his head in return. Gen turned her attention to the second man entering the diner. The deputy was a regular. "Good morning, Ken." She nodded to the dark-haired man that entered behind them. Her eyes traveled after the extremely tall and broad cowboy before she remembered Ken, who'd sat down in front of her. "Coffee?"

The deputy sheriff smiled and nodded. "Sounds good. Need a couple ham biscuits, too."

Gen plated his food quickly and made sure he was set before she took two cups of coffee over to Ryan and the tall cowboy that sat with him. She poured the strong, hot liquid from a decanter and filled the cups. "I am sorry to hear about you losing a cow last night, Ryan. Doc was in earlier and told me. Hope Senior wasn't too upset. How is the little guy that you managed to save?"

The old cowboy's eyebrows rose as he looked across the table at his companion. The man dipped his head and took a sip of his coffee before he reached for the sugar container on the table. Ryan chuckled a bit and answered, "Thanks, Gen, the little guy is fine. Put him on one of the other cows that delivered last night. I think Mr. Hollister understands it is the nature of the business."

Gen nodded. "Yeah, I guess. It is a shame to lose a good animal, though. Can I get y'all some breakfast or just coffee this morning?" Her Southern accent was almost nonexistent, but a couple of her colloquialisms still made the locals smile. 'Y'all' was one of those words.

Ryan swallowed a sip of coffee and nodded toward the counter. "I would love a caramel roll."

She looked across the table, smiling happily at the man with him. The quiet cowboy concentrated on his coffee. "You got it. And what can I get for you?" He shook his head and dropped his eyes to his coffee cup again. Weird, but hey, he might be a man of few words. She shrugged. "All right, one caramel roll coming up."

She filled a cup of coffee for one of her regulars before she made it into the kitchen and slid a massive roll onto a plate and warmed it in the microwave. With a tray of butter in hand, she popped back to the small table. "There you go. Let me know if you need more butter." She smiled at Ryan and nodded to the other ranch hand. Filling their cups again, she left a carafe at the table and moved back to the counter.

Andrew Hollister watched the woman in his peripheral vision as she went about her business. She was tall and curvy, and damn, she was beautiful. He cast another glance toward her. The woman had a bust line that would attract and hold any man's attention, but that wasn't what hooked him. No, it was her vivid, green-gold eyes. They were expressive and enchanting with thick, dark lashes circling them. No makeup, either. Her full lips and high cheekbones reminded him of one of the old-time movie stars he had watched with his grandmother when he was a kid. He stole another look as she wrote out something on a piece of paper and taped it to the door. She worked the counter, refilling cups and taking away plates before she bent over and rested her arms on the counter in front of Ken, who was now the local deputy.

Ken Zorn was a natural cop. Hell, the guy stood up for all the kids growing up and played referee whenever there was a disagreement.

Andrew gazed out the window and stared at the small town. *My town.* Yeah, that used to be such a point of pride for him. But it wasn't his town, it was Senior's. He'd left with the intention of never coming back, but time has a way of changing intentions. Well, time and war.

He took a sip of his coffee and glanced down the street. His old man had helped grow the hamlet his great-grandfather had founded. It was incorporated now and had a post office. Granted, it was just a small cubby of a place built onto the side of Sanderson's Market, but having a federal office out here was huge. The Marshalls had been the impetus for the recent growth, but his dad had taken care of everyone the way he always did. Senior was the font of kindness to strangers. Andrew dropped his eyes to his coffee. That kindness had never been cast his direction when he was growing up.

Gen laughed and pulled his attention back to the occupants of the diner. He hated being here, but he couldn't begrudge Ryan some breakfast. They'd worked all night and his ranch foreman's stomach was growling loudly when they dropped off the cow for processing.

From what his men had told him, Genevieve Wheeler had settled in Hollister just about the time he was sent overseas the first time. His gaze lowered to the owner of the diner's tight ass, and he jolted as his body reacted. He covered the shock by immediately moving to add sugar to his already-sweetened coffee. *That* was something he didn't need to think about. It would do him no good. She moved from customer to customer and laughed freely, visiting with most. She was every bit the woman his men's yapping had built her up to be. Andrew normally didn't listen to the gossip the ranch hands spread, but she had been talked about a lot, and now, he understood why.

Ryan finished his roll and licked his fingers. "You should have one of these rolls. Damn, they're good."

Andrew looked at his foreman and shook his head. "No, thanks. I need to get back to the ranch and get back to work."

"Always working. When are you going to take a day off? I mean, the ranch can survive one day of you not being there." Ryan leaned back in his chair and took a sip of his coffee.

"This week I'll take a day. I need to drive down to Rapid City. I have to meet with the lawyers for Dad and I have some business to do for the processing plant with the bank, so I'll leave the ranch about seven, that way I can get things done and get back before dark."

"That ain't a day off. You're going to be working the whole time." Ryan shook his head and took another drink of his coffee. "You going to see that doc when you head south?"

Andrew shook his head. Way to squash a semi-normal morning. Ryan opened his mouth to argue. Andrew leveled his stare at the man and stated emphatically, "No."

Ryan leaned over the table, keeping the conversation between the two of them, "Listen, Drew, I ain't one to preach, but you need some help with them nightmares. That doctor is supposed to help you. If you don't want to talk to that one, talk to Doc Wheeler here. Word is he's damn good."

"I've had enough of doctors. End of discussion." He put his cup down.

Ryan sighed and dropped back against his chair. "Maybe you should find yourself a woman to wear you out so you can sleep." Ryan nodded toward Gen. "What about that long, tall drink of water? Might be a real challenge, though, I hear she has turned down every eligible man in Butte County and half the men in Harding County." The old cowboy chuckled, obviously amused at the thought.

Drew shook his head although Ryan couldn't possibly understand his reason for avoiding people in general. He had one, and it was time to remind his friend of that fact. "Ryan, you need to mind your own business. You're my foreman, not my father."

Ryan scoffed at him. "I got the right to fuss over you, Mister Andrew. I have known you since you were in diapers. I worry about you and so does Senior although him saying anything along those lines would likely kill him. Nobody in their right mind works as hard as you do or sleeps less. Senior told me about you screaming in the middle of the night. Ain't right. You need to get that taken care of."

"There is no magic pill for this one, Ryan." Andrew

rose and dropped a ten-dollar bill on the table and growled, "Besides, who says I am in my right mind, old man?"

Ryan whooped with laughter and lifted away from the table, too. "That's what I'm saying."

Gen watched the ranch hand and Ryan leave her diner and nudged Ken. "The new hand out of the Hollisters is quiet."

Ken looked at her like she had three heads. "What new hand?"

"That guy." She nodded her head out toward the street.

Ken turned and did a double-take. "The guy with Ryan?"

"Yep."

"That isn't a hand. That is Andrew Hollister."

Gen's eyes darted to the four-wheel-drive truck and the man driving it. "The sixth?"

"Yup. You've met Senior, that's his son."

Gen shook her head. "Huh… I had no idea. The last gossip I heard was that he was *coming* home, not *at* home." The man held little resemblance to his father except for the height and build.

The deputy nodded. "Yeah, that was him. I saw him about three months ago."

"He hasn't been around town. The ladies of the

circle would have announced it to everyone." Gen filled Ken's cup with hot coffee and bounced down the counter to clear some plates and pick up money left for breakfast. She made the circle of her small diner and filled coffee cups and chatted before she ended up in front of Ken again.

Her curiosity got the better of her and she asked, "I promise not to tell Edna Michaelson, but why hasn't he come to town?"

Ken chuckled. "Edna is an old snoop. Did you hear Father Murphy put her in her place yesterday?"

"Heard it in person. Almost busted a gut laughing, but I managed to make it into the kitchen before I did."

Ken chuckled again, and then his demeanor shifted, turning serious. "I figure there's a reason he's avoiding people. There were rumors about what happened. I can't imagine what he went through over there, so I give him some leeway. I grew up with him. Back then, he used to be different, really laid back and easy to get along with. He joined the Marine Corps after college and ended up a commander of a RECON squad."

"Rumors about what?" Strange that she hadn't heard anything from the gossip group.

"Well, according to some of the news reports that were on television, he got caught up in a bad situation overseas somewhere. Most of his men were killed and he was tore up pretty bad."

"Television?" She blinked at him. "Why was he on television?"

"Had to do with a medal he was given. Anyway, he was laid up in the hospital in Germany for months and months before the Marine Corps brought him back to the States. He got that medal and then they discharged him from Walter Reed Hospital and sent him home. He is a good guy, just seen way too much. If he chooses to be alone, I'll respect that. I'm sure the Ednas of the world are the reason why he avoids town."

"No doubt. Thanks for the background, at least I won't put my foot in it around him."

"Meh, he probably won't be around much, so little to no chance of that happening." Ken lifted his coffee to his lips and took a large gulp.

"Gen, honey, can I get a refill?" The polite request from one of her regulars interrupted her conversation with Ken.

A smile spread across her face as she reached for the carafe of coffee. "Coming right up!"

CHAPTER 2

The drive from Belle Fourche to Hollister was a two-hour trip with nothing to see but buttes, grazing land, antelope, and the rare vehicle heading south. Andrew switched stations on the radio several times before turning the damn thing off. Alone in his truck with his thoughts was not something he'd ever volunteer for, but it seemed to be his lot today because the music KBFS was playing irritated the hell out of him for some reason.

The trip down to Rapid had been productive. He'd taken care of the business his father wanted him to handle. He drove to the VA and parked his truck outside the building where the psychiatrist's office was located. He couldn't force himself to go inside, though. The military was a huge fan of group therapy and drugs to manage issues. He didn't want to participate in either. Was he still having nightmares? Yes. Almost every night, he found himself back in that sand with Gunny. He reached for his phone and dialed the only number he knew by heart.

"Hey, Cap." Andrew smiled. Gunny called him Cap, which was short for Captain America, not just his rank. The joke stuck, and he'd been called that by all his men.

"Gunny. How are you holding up?"

There was a long sigh. "I'm managing. Bone cancer sucks. I strongly recommend you don't get it."

"I'll take your advice on that. Are they helping you?" By 'they,' he meant the VA, but Gunny knew who he was talking about.

"Yes and no. The docs are good. The situation sucks. Good days and bad."

"More good than bad, I hope?" He fucking hated that Gunny was sick. They'd found the cancer when he was admitted after their firefight. Gunny knew he wasn't feeling right, but he'd been gutting it out. The disease moved from flesh to bone. Now he was stage four.

"Meh, they're all kind of average."

"How is Corrie doing?" He really liked the gunny's wife. She took care of all of them when they were stateside. The whole platoon loved her and her cooking. Loved. Past tense. At least, for everyone except him and Gunny. As far as he knew, FNG was still in a corner of some mental ward overseas. The kid hadn't done well with what he'd seen that day.

"She's a trooper, she really is. This isn't easy for her."

"It isn't easy for anyone, Jose. I have to get through calving season, then I'll pop down and see you."

"How long's that?"

"Two months."

"All right. I figure I can make that," Gunny chuckled. "No promises, though."

"You better fucking make it. What are the doctors saying?"

"Ah, the rounds of chemo helped, radiation is ongoing. Just prolonging things now."

Andrew drew a breath. Gunny had told him when they'd visited about a week ago the cancer had spread. "Do you need me to be there? I'll leave tomorrow."

"What are you going to do, Cap? Wipe my butt for me? No offense, but I don't want you anywhere near my ass." Gunny's laugh put a smile on his face.

"And I don't want to be anywhere near it. But I'm being serious, Gunny. Do you need anything from me? Do you need me there? Money? Anything?"

"No, we're doing okay. Maybe I'll ask something of you in the future, but right now, we're handling it." His friend sighed. "Sucks knowing the end is coming."

"I offered to get you to another doctor. A private one." He had money his grandmother had left him, and he'd drain the account in a second if it gave Jose hope. If he needed to, he'd ask Senior for more money.

"If there were any chance of beating this enemy, I'd

take you up on it, Cap. But I've seen the scans. I'm holding off the advancement, but now it is about quality time with Corrie." Jose cleared his throat. "I'll see you in two months."

"I'll call soon."

"Damn, really?"

The feigned exasperation in the man's voice made Andrew laugh. "Really. You can't get rid of me, Gunny."

"I told them not to saddle me with you. Now look what I have to deal with."

"Bullshit, you begged for me."

"Begged? No, if I recall the conversation with the XO, it went something along the lines of, 'Sir, that country hayseed will get himself killed without someone taking care of him.'"

"You taught me how to survive, Gunny." Andrew had known the NCO would be his crutch from day one and he'd used Gunny to learn how to be the best officer he could become.

"You figured things out damn fast and you were a good leader. Do you miss it?" Jose's voice sounded distant with the last question.

"The Corps? Yes, but it wouldn't be the same. You're not there." More than anything, he missed the relationships he'd built in the Corps. Relationships he didn't have on the ranch. Gunny was more a father to him than Senior was, and Gunny was only ten years older than Andrew.

"You would have promoted yourself out of our

squad. I would have had to break in a new Zero and keep his ass alive through another dozen or so conflicts. But looks like neither of us are going to get that future. How's living with the cows and your stubborn old man going?"

"The cows are easy. Senior, well, we're a work in progress. The Corps and a certain gunnery sergeant made me the type of man he didn't expect when I came back. I think I've set him on his heels a couple times." *And stood up for myself like I never did before I joined the Corps.*

"You keep working at it. There's nothing more important than family. The ones you choose and the ones you were born to. Never let that go. That old man of yours is probably just waiting for you to come to him and clear the air."

"I'm pounding my head against that wall, Jose. I swear I'll clear the air, eventually."

"Well, good. Needs to be done. A lot of shit needs to be done. Don't wait until you're in my position to realize it. Carpe diem, Cap."

"I will."

"You found yourself a little filly, or do they call them heifers up there?" Gunny laughed and Andrew rolled his eyes.

"They're called women up here, and you know the military gave me a little complication where that's concerned."

"Fuck. Still can't…"

"Yeah, also a work in progress." He didn't want to go there with Gunny, but besides the docs, Jose was the only one who knew he couldn't get it up. Although, on occasion, his dick would twitch and act like it was going to come back to life, he hadn't been able to orgasm since he was shot.

"They said your plumbing was fixed, right?"

Andrew chuffed, "That's what they said."

"Then work it, son."

"I so do not want to talk about this with you." He could feel his face turning red.

"Who else you going to talk to? Seriously, have you tried to jerk off?"

"Jose…"

"Cap, I'm serious, have you?"

Andrew drove over a hill and saw a truck and trailer pulled off to the side of the road. "Hey Gunny, I'll call you back. Looks like someone has broken down. I'm going to see if I can help."

"Dude, do they do that up there? Stop for vehicles beside the road?"

Andrew decelerated and laughed. "Yep, and we still wave when we pass another vehicle."

"You live in the stone age."

"Sometimes, but people out here are the salt of the earth." He pulled off the road behind the truck and trailer, putting his truck into park. There was a jack with a lug wrench attached to the spare for the trailer, but nobody… *Oh, there she is.*

"Talk to you in a few days, Cap."

"You bet. Take care of yourself."

"As best as I can." Jose hung up, and Andrew checked his rearview before opening the door out of habit. There hadn't been anyone behind him for miles.

Genevieve Wheeler leaned back from the bed of the truck where she was digging in the mounted toolbox behind her cab. She shaded her eyes to look at him before she smiled widely. "Hey! Thanks for stopping. Would you happen to have anything I can use as a fulcrum? I have a locked lug nut on the trailer."

"I should. Hold on." He made his way to his toolbox and opened it. A long-handled crowbar would do the trick.

He walked back and placed the bar between the handles of the lug wrench and twisted it. The lug groaned but loosened.

"Oh, thank you so much. I have no idea what happened to my crowbar. Ten bucks my nephew borrowed it to work on his fort he's building behind my diner."

"No problem." Drew removed the stubborn lug and set it on the fender of the trailer and started to loosen the next one.

"I can do that. I don't expect you to change the tire."

"I'm here and I haven't changed a tire for a damsel in distress in years." Drew didn't look at her and he had no idea why he was flirting. His cock twitched the same way it had at the diner when he'd seen her the first time. He doubled his efforts on the next lug to keep his mouth shut and his mind busy. He didn't want to attribute his broken cock's interest as anything but what it was: coincidence.

"Okay, there are so many things wrong with that statement." Gen laughed.

He glanced up at her where she was leaning against her truck. "Oh yeah, like what?" So much for keeping his mouth shut.

"First, I haven't been a damsel since my debutante debut, and that was many years ago. Second, I'm not in distress, just inconvenienced, but if this is the worst thing that happens today, I'm good. And third... Well, I don't have a third, but I'll think of something."

Her laughter bubbled around him, and he smiled although he tried to hide it from her. He could like this woman, which was a good reason to avoid her, now, wasn't it?

"I haven't had a flat in years. It was due, I guess. Phil checks my tires before I go, but I left before he opened the garage this morning. I wanted to get back at a decent hour and I get a discount at the big box stores with my premium membership card if I'm there early. Are you heading back from Belle?"

He put another lug on the fender. "Yep." He grunted his reply. Another frozen lug. "Hand me the crowbar, please?"

She handed it to him, and he slipped it between the arms of the lug wrench and twisted. The damn thing was stuck hard. He shifted and strained against the resistance, gritting his teeth and willing his muscles to break the lock the metal had on the lugs. The bar moved slowly and then broke free. His hand went with the bar, and he scraped some skin off his knuckles. He grunted and examined his hand.

"Oh, shoot. Stop, I've got something for that."

"It's all right, it's nothing." He shook out the sting and unfastened the lug he'd broken free.

She didn't listen to him and was back with a water bottle, a piece of gauze, and a small, brown-colored container of some sort. "Here, let me get that cleaned up."

He stopped what he was doing and sat back on his heels. "I'm fine, thank you."

"Then just let me wipe off the blood and put some of this on. It won't take two minutes and it will make me feel better." She reached out and grabbed his hand. "Ouch. Yeah, let's get the dirt out of that."

He looked at the scrape, feeling the warmth of her hands as she examined the very superficial damage to his knuckles. She moved his arm out, stretching it toward the weeds at the side of the road. She emptied the entire bottle over the scrape while stopping occasionally to pick a bit of something off his skin.

"I really don't need…"

"I know, but you hurt yourself helping me. This damsel is all about first aid." She flicked those huge, green-gold eyes at him and smiled.

He let her continue with her ministrations but jerked when she applied whatever it was onto the scrape she'd dried. "Damn, is that straight alcohol?"

Gen winced. "I'm sorry, I should have warned you. It is a liquid bandage, and it does sting." She blew on his knuckles.

His cock jumped behind his zipper, and he pulled his hand away so he could hide the reaction his body was having. "Thanks."

"No problem." He heard her walk back to the cab of her truck while he took off the last lug nut which, thankfully, wasn't frozen onto the lug. It took five more minutes to replace the tire, replace the lugs, and lower the trailer. All of it was done in silence.

"Thank you so much. I want you to come by the diner. Your next meal is free."

He handed her the jack and lug wrench, which she stowed behind the seat in the cab of her truck.

"I appreciate the offer, but I don't get to town often."

She nodded. "Yeah, I figured, but whenever you do, I'd like to feed you. It's what I do. It makes me happy."

"Feeding people?"

"Yeah, weird, huh?" She shrugged.

Did he sense a vulnerability in her comment and actions? "Not weird. Nice." She wasn't weird. Not by a long shot. He bent down and picked up his crowbar. "I'll follow you to the turnoff for Hollister." He was heading that way anyway.

"Oh, thank you. I don't think that will be necessary. I should be okay."

Again, that small tremor in her voice. Why did she think she wasn't worth such little effort? Or was he reading her wrong? Hell, it had been forever since he'd talked to anyone but doctors and the hands at the ranch. Well, until the other night, but he'd cast that off as an anomaly that had obviously repaired itself. Neither the Guardians nor the Marshalls had called for help. He put the crowbar in his toolbox. "It's no problem. I refer back to that knight-in-shining-armor thing I have going on today. Have to do it or my tin suit may tarnish." Damn, he needed to shut the fuck up. He headed back to his truck.

"Hey, Andrew?" Genevieve's voice sounded tentative.

He stopped and turned around. She shoved her hands into her back pockets and kicked at a rock. "I really would like to make you some food as a thank you. If you don't want to be around the people at the diner, I live above it and I'm closed on Sundays. You should stop by on a Sunday."

He stared at her for a moment and then nodded. They both got into their trucks, and he followed her all the way to the turnoff, honked as she made the turn, and headed back to the ranch. So what if he had a stupid grin on his face the entire time?

CHAPTER 3

"I diot." Gen berated herself for the five hundredth time. "You should stop by," she mimicked herself and groaned again. "Stupid." She grabbed several bags out of the ice chest in her trailer and trudged into the diner and to the walk-in cooler.

Andrew Hollister was drop-dead handsome and a loner. What in the hell did she expect? An immediate yes to her offer? And then—*then*—what does she do? She went and used the conversation she'd had with Ken to try to make her offer more attractive to the man. Like he cared. "Stupid. Absolutely stupid."

"Talking to yourself is the first sign of dementia."

She spun and narrowed her eyes. Her brother was leaning against the walk-in cooler's door.

"Is it really?"

"No, but I like messing with you." He smiled and bent down, picking up the bag with lettuce. "Do you need help with the groceries or thinking up synonyms for the word stupid?"

"Yes to the groceries and no to the word search, I'm doing just fine on my own." She put the tomatoes she'd bought onto the shelf and erased the old date on the dry erase board, putting the new shelf date on it.

"What's got you so upset?" Jeremiah put the heads of lettuce on the shelf, and she changed that date, too.

"I was just an idiot. Why are you over here? No more patients today?" She walked out of the cooler and out to the trailer.

Jeremiah followed her. "Actually, I'm meeting with someone, but they're delayed. I saw you pull in and thought you might need some help. How were you an idiot?" They both loaded up and trudged back inside the diner.

"I had a flat on the trailer and the lug nuts froze. I didn't have my crowbar, which I need to talk to your son about. I think he took it out of my truck to use it on his fort."

"I'll have a talk with him about putting things back where he got them. How did you get your tire changed?"

"Andrew Hollister stopped and changed it for me."

"Senior? That's... nice."

"Not Senior. The sixth." She stocked another shelf with cheese.

"You met him?"

She stopped and looked over her shoulder at him. "Yeah? Have you met him?"

"In passing the other night. Things were rather hectic, but yeah, he was there." Her brother stopped stocking the cartons of eggs she'd bought and cocked his head. "What could you have possibly done to call yourself or him stupid?"

"Oh, it's me that's stupid. I thanked him and asked him to come by so I could feed him, you know, to show him my appreciation."

Jeremiah straightened and stared at her. "I'm still waiting for the stupid part."

Gen groaned. "Ken Zorn told me in confidence that Andrew preferred to be away from town because of what happened overseas or something. But, instead of leaving it as an open invitation, I may have mentioned that I understood if he didn't want to be down in the diner and that I was closed on Sunday, so he should come over then and I'd cook for him." She rushed the words out, hoping they didn't sound as ridiculous to Jeremiah as they did to her.

Remi lowered his chin and narrowed his eyes. "I'm still waiting for the stupid part."

"That was the stupid part! He didn't need to be reminded that he didn't like crowds. I'm such an idiot."

Jeremiah grunted and picked up the cloth bag that was now empty. "I don't think it was stupid. Accommodating and forward, yes. Stupid, not even close."

Gen's head snapped up. "Forward?" She rolled her eyes heavenward. "I can't win."

"What do you want to win? Andrew?" Her brother's question stopped her reaction in its tracks.

"What?" Her voice rose an octave or two.

Jeremiah smiled at her. "You like him?"

"This isn't grade school, Remi." She picked up an empty bag and folded it, shoving it onto the shelf where it belonged.

"Okay, then how about... are you attracted to him?"

She threw her brother a withering look. "Are you going to help?"

"I said I would." His laughter followed her out of the kitchen.

"How are things out at the Marshall Ranch?" She grabbed one end of a crate that held the Sandersons' order and Jeremiah grabbed the other. They walked back to the kitchen.

"Fine. Why do you ask?"

"Because something happened, and you know it."

"Do I?"

She grunted as they put the crate down. "I don't want to know what happened, I just want to know if everyone is okay."

Her brother's eyes met hers. He nodded once. "Do you need help with anything else?"

Gen shook her head. "I'll call Allison to come get this and then I'm prepping for tomorrow. Oh, wait." She jogged to the truck and opened the cab. "This is for

Jay, but tell him I want it back because I haven't watched it yet."

Jeremiah grabbed the DVD. "Wow, thanks. I planned on picking this up for him, but I've lost track of the date the last couple of days."

"Yeah, it's been a week, right? Anyway, it released yesterday." The superhero movie franchise was making a mint off her, but she loved them as much as Jay and Remi did.

"Thanks, and seriously, you didn't make a fool of yourself. If you like this guy, it's okay." Remi grabbed her and pulled her in for a hug. "Let yourself be happy, Gen."

She pulled away and shook her head. "I tried that once, remember?"

Jeremiah snorted. "Avery was Mom's choice, not yours."

"It took me a while to realize that, and just for your information, he still is." She made a face and explained when his eyebrows scrunched in confusion. "Mom gave him my address. It seems after all these years he wants to make amends. That, and Dad is going to make a run for President in six years, and the Montagues believe the ax should be buried between us."

Remi blinked and then shook his head. "You know, there is so much packed into that statement that needs to be analyzed. Starting with Dad making the decision to run and ending with Mother and the Montagues."

"Right? I'm surprised she hasn't called you."

"She has, several times. I just let it go to voicemail. I'll call her back when I have time." Remi walked with her to the kitchen.

"She's scheming again. I can feel it." Gen shivered as a chill ran up her spine.

"Always. I'll call her this weekend and see what she'll confess to."

"Thank you, and good luck."

"Don't mention it. I'll see you tomorrow for lunch." Jeremiah winked at her and left. Gen sighed and closed her eyes.

Her brother was such a balm for her nerves. She pulled out her phone and called Allison.

While she waited for her friend to arrive, she retrieved a bottle of water and sat down. Her emotions were all over the place. Forward? Well, yeah, her invitation was forward. Why had she felt the need to let him know she knew he didn't like a crowd? Lord, she was attracted to the man. Yes, she'd definitely noticed his bulging muscles, and he wasn't hard to look at. That strong chin and straight nose, the dark brown hair, and that smile—when he let it appear—was breathtaking. So… yes, she was attracted.

Wow. She couldn't recall the last time she'd found herself attracted to someone. She leaned forward and dropped her head onto her crossed arms. Why now? Why him? She didn't need this complication in her life.

Her head snapped up, and she laughed. Good Lord, next thing you know, she'd be writing Andrew Hollister's name on her notebook and circling it with hearts. The man was a loner, and he wasn't going to show up for a meal. She really needed to get over herself.

"Knock, knock," Allison called out from the back door. Gen got up and headed to the door, to her real life, not the fairy tale version she'd concocted in her brain.

CHAPTER 4

Andrew wrote another item on the list of things they needed from the hardware store. They needed a tow strap, more roofing nails to finish replacing the shingles on the smaller barn, a couple of new shovels, and a handle for the pitchfork he'd broken this morning. The old, dry wood couldn't handle the weight of the shit he was slinging and had snapped in his hand so he'd finished mucking out the barn with a shovel.

"What are you doing?" Senior's voice behind him turned him.

"Making a list of things we need from the hardware store. I'll run in and get them."

"It's Sunday." His father crossed his arms over his chest. "You worked all night last night."

He folded the paper and put it into his pocket. "That's why I wrote everything down. I didn't want to forget anything."

"It can wait. You should get some sleep."

Yeah, that is so not going to happen. When he did sleep it was because exhaustion claimed him. At least, until the dreams woke him up again. "I'm good. Smokey's dropped a bit. I think she'll deliver in the next day or so." The horse was a beautiful Arabian mare that was bred to a champion stallion. His father's doing, but Andrew loved working with the horses.

"Reckon that's about right. Artificial insemination makes it easier to calculate the dates. You need keys to the hardware store?"

"Are they still in the lockbox?" He nodded to the metal box behind his father's desk.

"Yup." Andrew headed that way. Senior cleared his throat. "I'm worried about you, boy."

Andrew stopped in his tracks and turned to face his father. "Sir, I stopped being a boy the day I entered the Marine Corps."

His father's head came up quickly. "You'll always be my boy, no matter how old you get. You don't sleep. It will catch up with you one day."

"I sleep when I can. Thank you for your concern, but I'm managing." He was done talking about it. He turned and walked to the lockbox and opened it, grabbing the keys to the hardware store from the back hook. "Still just leaving a note for Carson to bill us?"

Senior nodded in response to Andrew's question.

"Managing." His dad grunted the word. "Ain't no way to live."

Andrew stared at the keys in his hands for a moment before he answered. "I'm alive. Most of my platoon isn't. What right do I have to even exist, let alone manage?"

His father blinked at him. "It's not your fault."

Andrew shook his head and ground his teeth together. If one more person told him what happened wasn't his fault, he was going to lose it. It wasn't a matter of *fault*, it was a matter of *responsibility*. "I respectfully disagree with your assessment, sir. They were my men. All of them should have survived that mission. If you'll excuse me, I need to get into town before church releases." He didn't want to run into anyone, even Carson. He also didn't wait to hear what else his father had to say. He couldn't right now. He was too damn tired. Senior's turn toward nurturing was awkward for both of them. Their dynamic was off kilter. Before the Marine Corps, he wouldn't have thought of disagreeing with his old man. Now, he didn't have any fucks left to give, so he stood his ground. Which was probably what had caused Senior's shift in attitude. He'd sit down and talk to his father later, but right now he needed space, and a drive to Hollister would give him that cushion.

He rolled down the windows of his truck and let the wind rush through the cab. If only the torrent of air could sweep away the exhaustion of the present and the guilt of the past. He pulled into the small town, passing the Catholic church, noting the parking lot was still full. He glanced at the clock on his dashboard. He had a good half hour before people would shake hands with Father Murphy and wander back to their cars or homes.

He pulled down the side street and parked behind the hardware store. Leaving the back door open, he went in search of what they needed.

"Hey, mister, do you know if Mister Schmidt will be here today?"

Andrew turned at the question. The young boy standing at the back door had wild hair, dirty jeans, and a streak of some kind of dirt or mud on his cheek. "Doubtful as it's Sunday."

The boy shoved his hands into his pockets and sighed dramatically. "Dang it."

"Can I help you with something?"

His eyes lit up. "I need a crowbar. One about this big. I have two dollars and twenty-seven cents. Is that enough?" The boy held out his hands, showing Andrew how long the crowbar needed to be.

"Why do you need a crowbar?"

"I borrowed my Aunt Gen's and I can't find it. Dad is really *not* happy with me. She got a flat tire, and if some guy hadn't stopped to help her, she'd have been stranded. I'm supposed to be looking for it while Mom and Dad are at church, but I've looked everywhere and can't find it."

49

"Ah." Andrew nodded. "I understand. Let's go see what we have." The boy jogged after him. "Which size?" Andrew touched three different sizes of bars hanging from pegs on the wall.

"That one." The kid pointed to the middle size. "How much is it?"

Andrew picked up the bar and tore off the price tag. "Two dollars even."

"Awesome!" The boy shoved his hand into his pocket and pulled out two old, crumpled dollar bills, handing them to Andrew. Taking the money, Andrew handed him the bar. "Thanks, mister." A shout as the young boy ran out of the store put a smile on his face. He'd add the cost of the crowbar to his bill.

Andrew wrote out a note to Carson and added a few things he remembered they needed as he pulled items from the shelf. Gathering his equipment together, he turned off the lights in the front of the store.

"Hello?"

Andrew stopped and jerked his head up. Gen Wheeler stood at the door. Beside her was the young man who'd bought the crowbar. "Hello."

"Oh, hi. Jay here said he bought this from you?" She held up the crowbar.

"He did. Seems he's in some hot water for losing one." Andrew suppressed a smile when the kid sighed.

"He is, but he was supposed to find the one he lost, not buy his way out of the situation."

"But, Aunt Gen, I can't find it! I searched everywhere!" The boy pleaded his case.

"Have you? Behind your fort?"

"Yes."

"In the shed?"

"Yes, ma'am."

"In the back of the trailer?" She crossed her arms.

"The trailer?" The boy's face scrunched. "Oh!" He sprinted away from the building.

"I found it as I was reconstituting the trailer after I unloaded it. I left it where it was so he could find it." She handed the crowbar back to Andrew.

He took it and put it on Carson's desk. "Thanks, I'll mark it off the list and you can give your nephew back this." He pulled the crumpled two dollars out of his pocket.

Gen laughed and held up the ragged paper. "Can this even be considered legal tender?"

"It bought a crowbar, so I think it passes."

"That's true."

"Aunt Gen! I found it!" The boy's exuberant yell came from outside.

Gen leaned back and yelled, "Awesome, bud, put it back in the cab of my truck, okay?"

"Okay!" the reply came immediately.

"Are you heading back to the ranch, or could I interest you in some shrimp creole for lunch?"

"Shrimp creole?" He parroted her because the invitation took him by surprise.

"Yep. Good, down-home southern cooking. I don't make this version for the diner. The shrimp is too expensive up here. I like to keep my prices on the lower end of the scale." She crossed her arms and leaned against the door jamb. "Unless you have to head back to the ranch."

He looked down at the items he had gathered. There was no way he was going to get out of this gracefully, was there? "Yeah, I should head back."

"Okay. I understand. Enjoy your day." She pushed away from the door.

Andrew nodded and blinked as she smiled hesitantly before she walked away. *Well, hell.* He drew a deep breath. Why did he feel like shit for turning her down?

Gen shook her head as she headed back home. If that rejection didn't put her in her place, nothing would. She was over extending any invitations to the guy. It was obvious his lone-wolf drive was strong, and she wasn't going to entice the wolf to her door with food. Whatever. She'd given it the ol' college try.

A truck crunched down the driveway, pulling her attention from Andrew Hollister. She waved at Eden as Jeremiah pulled the truck behind her building. Eden waved back but stayed in the truck when Jeremiah parked it. The blanket over her shoulder explained the reason why. Carmen was nursing.

"I found the crowbar, Dad!" Jay exclaimed as he raced toward his father.

"Did you? That's fantastic. Did you apologize to Aunt Gen for misplacing it?"

"I did."

"And why do we put things back from where we get them?" Jeremiah high-fived his son as the boy made it to him.

"So we know where it is the next time we need it." Jay parroted the answer his father had undoubtedly impressed upon him.

"Hey, Jay, come here for a minute." Gen bent down to the boy's level when he made it to her. She handed him the money he'd given Andrew out of his father's view. "You forgot to get a refund." She lifted an eyebrow.

The boy's face split into a wide smile as he grabbed his worn money. "Cool. Thank you!"

"No problem. Now, get gone, you wild thing." She laughed as he raced back to the truck.

"Are you coming out for dinner tonight?" Jeremiah asked as he opened the rear door for Jay.

"Rain check. I'm going to watch the movie Jay brought back for me and go to bed early."

"I'll swing by tomorrow for coffee." Jeremiah got back into the truck.

"See you then." She waved and watched her family

pull out. With a sigh, she headed back up to her apartment.

The tomato and mirepoix base for her shrimp creole smelled amazing as soon as she opened her door. It had been simmering in a dutch oven for two hours, filling her small apartment with the heavenly aroma. All she had to do was add the shrimp for a couple minutes to cook them through and then pour the deliciousness on top of the jasmine rice she'd made. She glanced at the movie on her counter. A perfect distraction for the afternoon.

A knock on her back door forced a snort from her. She shouted from the kitchen, "What did you forget this time, young man?" When there was no reply, she walked to the back door.

Andrew Hollister gave her an awkward smile. "Is that invitation still open?"

"Absolutely." She unlatched the screen door and stepped back, inviting him in. As he passed her, she once again realized how broad and tall the man was.

"Have a seat. It will take me just a couple minutes to dish it up. How is calving season going?"

Andrew pulled out a chair and sat down, removing his cowboy hat and placing it on the chair beside him. "The cows seem to deliver when the sun goes down, but besides that, only a few problems."

"I've heard that from the hands and ranchers that come in." Gen grabbed a large bowl of shrimp she'd deveined and cleaned earlier and slid them into the thick, spicy stew to cook. "I figure it's the lady cows' way of paying you back for making them have a baby every year or so."

Andrew chuckled. "It very well could be. Ryan said you've lived here for several years?"

"Yep. I bought the business right after a nasty breakup. I was looking for someplace that my past wouldn't follow me and a place that I could be myself."

"Hollister let you do that?" He leaned back in the chair as she put down the silverware.

"It was the absolute best decision I've ever made. I love it here." She ladled two bowls half-full of rice and lifted the lid on the dutch oven. The shrimp were pink all the way through. She ladled his bowl full and then put a smaller amount in hers. She set the bowl in front of him and headed to the refrigerator. "I have water, lemonade, beer, or soda. I'm having a beer, the creole is spicy."

"I'll take a beer and a water, please." Andrew leaned over the creole and inhaled. "It smells fantastic. The farthest south I ever made it was Paris Island."

"Where's that?" Gen pulled two beers and two waters from the fridge and placed them on the table. "Oh, I have some of Mrs. Sanderson's sourdough rolls." She got the rolls and the butter and put them on the table, too.

"Thank you for this." Andrew motioned to the table.

"Thank you for stopping by. I like to cook." She picked up her spoon. "Where is Paris Island?"

"South Carolina."

"You were in the Army?"

Andrew almost choked on the food he'd put in his mouth. She reached over and slapped him between the shoulders. He shook his head and took a swig of his beer. "Marine." The word came out through a strangled cough.

"Oh. Sorry?" She looked at him, hoping an apology was what he wanted.

He cleared his throat and laughed. "Generally speaking, Marines think they're superior to the Army."

"Really? What about the Navy and the Air Force?" She took a bite of the dish. The flavors burst on her tongue, and she was happy that he'd taken her up on the invitation. She'd outdone herself today.

Andrew chuckled and took another bite. "Them too. This is freaking amazing." He spooned another bite into his mouth.

"Thank you. I splurged on the shrimp. Back home, we used to have shrimp boils with forty or fifty pounds of shrimp, corn on the cob, small potatoes, spicy andouille sausage, the works. Our picnic tables had holes in the middle so we could push the shells into a garbage can. The fresh seafood is about the only thing I miss from living there." She broke a roll in half and buttered the crusty bread. "Did you like the military?"

Andrew shrugged and buttered a roll for himself. "I liked the people. The relationships."

"That's what I meant when I said I love it here. The

relationships. You can't find a better place to live than this little town."

Andrew took another bite but didn't agree with her. She backed off the subject and took a bite, giving him the opportunity to carry the conversation.

"How did you find Hollister?"

"Oh, well, that was an adventure in and of itself. Like I said, I was escaping a situation that swore me off men for the rest of my life. No offense."

His brows flew up. "None taken."

She laughed and stirred her creole a bit as she spoke, "My dad wanted me to go to the Med to get away. My mother demanded I apologize to my cheating ex-fiancé and fix things up. I went a bit crazy, got in my car, and drove north. I took a left before I hit Lake Michigan and kept driving. When I realized I was in South Dakota, I went to see the faces and then wandered through the hills. I drove north again, and my radiator died on me about three miles south of town. I limped into town and Phil took care of me. While he was fixing the leak, I wandered around. I saw this place all boarded up and looking lonely." She stopped and looked to her right and to her left. "I went around back, and the door was open. I snuck in and inspected the place."

"Breaking and entering?" Andrew's eyebrows raised, and a smile appeared.

"We won't tell Ken, and officially, I don't think it was breaking, but it was entering. I saw so much potential in this little place, and when the realtor said the apartment was part of the deal... well, I was hooked. Although the clause about a lifetime lease on the land was confusing." She popped a piece of bread into her mouth and smiled as she chewed.

"My great-grandfather started that. The town wasn't a sustainable operation to begin with, so he enticed people to settle by giving them a lifetime lease on the land. When they pass, their heirs have the option to renew, but they seldom do. This town isn't a winning proposition for young people. Unless they're ranchers." Andrew finished his sourdough roll, and she pushed the plate with the rest toward him. He took another one and split it open.

"Sounds like goodness runs in your family."

He shrugged again. "What about yours?"

"Ah, mine? Well, you've probably met my brother, Jeremiah, right?"

Andrew stopped chewing. "I have. How did he end up here? Before or after you?"

"Oh, man, that would be after. Haven't you heard about the serial killer that came to town?"

Andrew put down his spoon and looked at her. "Say what, now?"

Gen's eyes grew wide. "Oh, man, buckle up. I can't believe you didn't hear about this..."

Andrew laughed hard at Gen's impersonation of Father Murphy. "I'm telling you, it was everything I could do to make it into the kitchen before I laughed, and I'm pretty sure I didn't do a very good job muffling it. Edna didn't leave me her normal fifty-cent tip."

"She's been an old snoop my entire life. I think she's a relic from a bygone era. That woman lives to stir the shit. Excuse my French."

Gen waved him off. "Thank you for that, but if I'm being honest, I've said worse, and I agree with you. That team of busybodies will drag anyone through the dirt. I don't know how they survive without a little drama or angst to feed their gossip addiction."

"This was very good, thank you for inviting me. Can I help with the dishes?" Andrew hated to end the conversation, but they'd been done with lunch for over an hour. It was time he headed back to the ranch.

"No, it will give me something to do this afternoon. Well, that and my date with a superhero."

Andrew blinked. "What?"

She smiled and grabbed a DVD off the countertop. "I let Jay watch it first. He has me hooked."

Andrew took the DVD from her and chuckled. "Gunny's addicted to these."

"Gunny?"

Andrew snapped his mouth shut. *Shit*.

"Hey, it's okay. No pressure. If you want to watch it after me, it's all yours although Jay will want it back eventually. He and his dad have movie marathons."

Andrew nodded. "Thanks, I'll keep that in mind." He wasn't going to watch it. He wasn't going to watch anything that had guns, explosions, or death in it, no matter how good the good guy was. "But I really should be going."

"Well, thank you for coming by. If you're around next Sunday, I'll be here." She followed him to the door.

He smiled and nodded. As enjoyable as the last hour... no, two and a half hours had been, he doubted he'd be back. "Again, thank you."

She smiled and watched as he walked down the stairs. At the bottom, he gave a casual wave and headed to his truck which was still parked behind the hardware store. As he drove home, a smile spread. For a small time today, he'd felt normal. There were a few moments that were uncomfortable, but Genevieve Wheeler was vivacious, funny, and somehow knew when they'd strayed too close to uncomfortable topics.

The afternoon filled itself with mundane tasks, calving checks, and frequent stops to see Smokey. The mare was getting ready to foal, but it could happen anytime in the next week. He made sure to let Ryan know as the man headed out for his turn to check the herd.

His father wasn't around when he came in, so he made himself a sandwich and ate it over the sink. He cleaned up and headed to his side of the house. His father's master suite took the left side of the house, Andrew's room was on the right.

His clothes were tossed into the hamper for the housekeeper to deal with, and he stepped into the shower. Warm water hit his exhausted muscles. Damn, it felt good. He lathered the bar of soap and washed his face, chest, and back. When his hand brushed his cock, the thing kicked like it was a month-old colt, frisky but not capable of doing much of anything. He soaped his balls and his cock filled.

Andrew closed his eyes and dropped his head back against the tile. *All right, let's get it over with.* He looked down at the cock in his hand. "You know this will end in frustration, and so do I." Andrew barked out a laugh. *You're talking to your dick.* The laughter ended when he slid a soapy hand down his shaft. He groaned at the feeling of blood filling his cock. The doctors had told him to jerk off, to 'get back on the horse,' but to what end? The shrink he'd seen twice said that perhaps his interest in sex would come back when he stopped blaming himself for...

Andrew groaned and dropped his hand as his cock deflated. *Way to go, Hollister. Only you could fuck up a wet dream.*

He rinsed, dried, and padded into his bedroom where he pulled back the covers and fell into bed. His eyes closed only because he couldn't keep them open any longer.

CHAPTER 5

Andrew turned and watched Frisco, Team One's leader, walk toward the door of the shack they were clearing. They'd worked damn hard today. He and Gunny were along with the team because they were on a deep reconnaissance maneuver. The extra eyes and talent were needed, and he and Gunny supplied it because the other two teams in the platoon were strapped with their own requirements.

Gunny appeared by his side. "What do you see?"

"What?" He glanced over at his mentor and friend. Their position changed. They were inside the shack.

"What do you see, Cap? Are you going to stop this?"

Andrew's head snapped toward the door. The door his entire fucking team was approaching. The trip wire glistened in the desert sun. His warning shout echoed at the same time the bomb's percussion hit him. The initial blast threw him past a small half-wall, stopping huge pieces of shrapnel from entering his upper body. His lower body was pierced by *flaming metal shards, sending white-hot bolts of pain through his groin. Everything went black until he heard the ringing in his ears from the explosion. The high-pitched whine muted the sounds of small arms fire, deafening the noise until the shots sounded like popcorn popping. Voices screamed, and the stench of sulfur and blood filled his nostrils. He cast through the gore. The bodies of his men lay lifeless, torn, and bloody. Pieces of them were strewn through the rubble. Drew tried to reach them, he tried to help, but he couldn't seem to make his body move. Why couldn't he move?*

He woke with a start, terrified and panting like a wild animal. The sheets of his bed were drenched with perspiration. His eyes wildly searched the room, trying to orient his racing mind to reality. He tried to still his harsh breathing. *The dream. Again.* Every time he slept. This dream or different variations of the damn thing. Drew closed his eyes momentarily, willing his body to relax, but no amount of cajoling himself would work. He'd been here too many times to count.

He whipped off the covers, jumped under an ice-cold shower, and dressed. Letting himself out of the house, he made his way to the barn and checked on Smokey. The horse lifted its head and huffed at him. He made sure she was okay and then leaned against the stall wall. His nerves jumped under his skin like little bursts of lightning, bouncing from his arms to his legs and back again. He needed to move.

Finding himself at his truck, he got in and started it

up. He rolled down both windows and pulled out of the ranch. The cool air slid across his skin. The soothing sensation and the darkness before the dawn worked. He drew a deep breath and turned onto the interstate. The sensation of being electrocuted a nerve ending at a time slowly ebbed. He could head back home and relieve whoever had the early morning watch on the herd.

He pulled into Hollister and drove down the street, intending on making a U-turn past Phil Granger's garage. He glanced to the right and saw the light of the diner on and Genevieve standing in the window. He pulled in, killed the lights, and got out of the truck.

The smile on her face was brilliant and immediate. She flicked the lock open and pushed the door wide. The bells above the door chimed excitedly. "To what do I owe this pleasure? Oh, crap. Did you lose another cow?"

Andrew shook his head. "No, actually, I couldn't sleep and went for a drive."

Gen blinked. "Oh. Well, damn."

Andrew stopped with his hat halfway off his head. "Damn?"

"Yeah, I'm trying to figure out if I should offer you coffee. Are you going to go back to sleep, or are you up for the day?"

He finished taking off his hat. "I'm not going back to sleep." At least, not until he was exhausted and couldn't stay awake any longer.

"Then coffee it is. I have caramel rolls baking. They are amazing fresh out of the oven."

"Both, please." He sat at the counter, and she moved behind it. The coffee was hot, fresh, and just as good as it was the last time he was here. He made a move to reach for the sugar, but she beat him to it and handed it to him.

"You like yours sweet?"

"No offense, but it is the only way I can drink it."

"None taken. My grandma put so much milk and sugar in hers that it turned white and made my teeth ache. You like what you like. Never apologize for that."

He added some sugar and stirred it with a spoon that appeared before him. "Thank you."

"You're welcome. I love this time of the morning. Before the day starts for the rest of the world. I feel this utter contentment and peace." She picked up her cup and leaned against the back counter. "The day hasn't started, and it holds such promise."

Andrew blinked at her. "Are you always this chipper?"

She laughed. "Most of the time. According to my brother, it's a serious character flaw, and he's suggested therapy several times. But hey, own what you are, right?"

He chuckled. "I guess. Are you up this early every morning?"

"Every morning. Sundays I sit on my back porch

and watch the sun come up. I've always been an early riser. You?"

"Since the military, sleep isn't easy." He dropped his eyes to his coffee. *Now why in the hell did you say that?*

"I couldn't begin to imagine." He glanced up at her. There was no pity or judgement, just her stating a simple fact.

"You wouldn't want to. It was difficult."

"You said you miss the people and relationships from the military. Do you keep in contact with anyone? A lady Marine perhaps?" She lifted away from the counter when a bell rang in the kitchen.

He snorted. "No, there isn't anyone like that. I do keep in contact with one person. My gunny."

She stopped and glanced out the passthrough to the kitchen. She lifted up two huge, insulated potholders and asked, "Excuse me, your what now?"

He rose and followed her into the kitchen, stopping just inside the door. "My gunnery sergeant for the platoon. He taught me how to be an officer."

She looked over at him as she withdrew a huge sheet of rolls from the oven. "The Marine Corps didn't do that for you?"

He laughed, a genuine, heartfelt laugh. "They taught me enough to be dangerous to myself and others. Jose taught me to lead, how to take care of my men, give them high cover, and how to stand my ground when the brass over us was being stupid. He is probably the strongest man I've ever met."

"Is he still in the Marine Corps?"

He watched her flip the pan over onto a larger sheet pan. She lifted the pan, and the caramel at the bottom oozed between the layers of cinnamon sugar and yeast roll. His grandmother had made rolls like that for him before she passed. "No. He was injured and is out now."

She looked up at him. "Sorry. I didn't mean to bring back any bad memories."

He shook his head. "You didn't. Jose brings up nothing but good thoughts." Except for his cancer, but that was something the man was fighting.

"You ready for a roll?"

"Sure." He watched her slice out a huge piece and put it on a plate.

"Butter?"

"Of course. And milk, if you have it."

"There you go. That's the spirit. Take this. I'll get us some milk."

He made his way back to the front of the diner and parked it on his stool. She came out with two glasses and a smaller roll for herself. She sat down beside him. "I don't usually eat until after the morning crowd has gone. There's a lull when I'm cooking lunch and I'll grab something then. This is a treat. Thank you for stopping by."

"I'll have to do it more often." Damn his stupid mouth and lack of a filter. He shoved a piece of the roll into his mouth and damn near burnt every taste bud he had off when the hot sugar hit his tongue.

She blew on her roll before she put it into her mouth. Smart woman. He blinked back the tears that welled in his eyes and chugged his glass of milk.

"Just a word of warning. Things that come out of the oven may be hot." She got up, snatched his empty glass, and laughed as she walked into the kitchen. "I'll get you more milk. And B.T.W., I'd like you to stop by more often, too."

He smiled and shook his head. She was a handful, that woman.

Andrew had no legitimate excuse to find his way into town yet again this morning. Hell, they were up to their necks in work at the ranch, but here he was at four-fifteen in the morning, pulling up to the diner in Hollister. He sat in his truck a second. What could actually come of this... hell, what did they have? A friendship? Because as much as he'd like to deny it, the woman was probably his only friend in the state. Or the Tri-State region, for that matter.

He'd even followed the doctor's orders. He wasn't fully functional, he hadn't orgasmed, but he got hard and stayed that way. On the verge between pain and pleasure, his mind would sabotage his body's need. Hell, he was broken. She didn't deserve that, did she?

He rubbed his face and grabbed his cowboy hat. That was putting the horse about two miles before the cart. He still hadn't gotten up the nerve to ask her out. And where would out be? They'd have to drive over two hours to a restaurant that wasn't hers.

He got out of his truck and ambled to the front door of the diner. Gen was in the kitchen, but when she saw him, she jogged to the door and let him in. "Are we going for a record? Three times last week and four times this week?"

"I guess you'll have to blame your coffee and food, they're addicting." He walked over to the stack of coffee cups and grabbed one. He noticed a crate of peppers, onions, and celery on the far workstation. "What's on the lunch menu for today?"

"Jambalaya. You really have to try it. So good, if I do say so myself."

"I doubt I'll be in town at lunchtime."

"Then come back for dinner. It gets better the longer it sits."

"Tempting."

"Well, dang, I hope so." She laughed. "I keep hoping there is something besides the food and coffee that keeps you coming back. Like my engaging personality or bubbly disposition." She yelled the later part as she moved into the back part of the kitchen. He followed her with his cup to the urn of coffee that she was brewing in the kitchen.

"That might have something to do with it." He gave her a half-smile when she craned her neck to see him.

"Did that hurt?"

He frowned. "Did what hurt?"

"Admitting you *might* like me?" She belted out a laugh and pulled out a tray of thick, fluffy biscuits. "I think I need to build a coop and buy chickens. Laying hens."

"Why?" He watched her work, knowing from trying before that getting in her way to help was a no-go from the start.

"I want to start putting eggs on the breakfast sandwiches, made to order, of course." She took off the mitts and grabbed the brush and melted butter.

"And you need a coop to do that?"

"I don't, but if I had my own source, I could cut down expenses."

"Chickens and a massive garden plot. Industrious." She'd shown him the huge garden that had been planted this spring. She was going to be busy when the crop started coming in. But then again, it seemed she was always working.

"I try. My degree in business may have something to do with me wanting to cut out the middleman." She chuckled. "Brown University would be so impressed with their summa cum laude graduate right now."

He whistled. "Brown, huh? Impressive."

She snorted. "In my past life, I would have agreed with you. Now, it's just a piece of paper and experience that provided the fundamentals I use to run this little place."

"What did you do in Birmingham?"

"I worked at Montague, Harding, and Bassett. It was a law firm, but I was the firm's business manager. HR, payroll, accounts receivable and payable. You know, I kept the wheels going."

"Sounds important."

She shook her head. "You'd think, right? I was miserable. I didn't realize *how* miserable until I left."

Andrew sipped his coffee. Damn, he needed sugar. "Why did you leave?"

"The impetus, you mean? I was engaged to this guy, Avery Montague. He was a junior partner in the firm but would take over for his father eventually. We were one of those power couples, you know?" She rolled her eyes. "Anyway, I made the fortunate mistake of going home sick one day."

Andrew cocked his head. *Wait, what?* "Being sick is a fortunate mistake?"

"Well, no. Let me rephrase that. I went home sick and found my fiancé screwing my best friend in my bed. I was fortunate because I found out what an egg-sucking dog he was, no offense to any dogs of the world."

Andrew pulled out a stool near the counter where she was working. "What happened to the best friend?"

"She married him and then divorced him. Seems he cheated on her. Who would have imagined that, right?" Gen laughed ruefully and shook her head.

"Sounds like you dodged a bullet."

"Several. You really have no idea." She glanced around the kitchen. "Caramel, cinnamon, or a biscuit this morning?"

"Dealer's choice." He picked up his cup as she grabbed two plates.

"I'm having a ham biscuit. Sausage, right?"

"That works. Milk?" He sat his coffee cup down and grabbed two glasses.

"Yes, please. How's calving going?"

"Pretty good this year. Don't tell anyone I said so, but Senior's new artificial insemination program is working well." He poured them each a glass of milk and followed her to the counter where they ate.

"Why wouldn't you tell someone you said that? It was a compliment. Thank you." She took the glass from him and took a sip of her milk.

"Senior and I have a rocky relationship. He was strict while I was growing up. Old school, I guess you'd say. I never measured up, no matter what I did. Always could do better. I lived my life knowing I was a disappointment to the old man."

Gen stared at him. "Is that why you left?"

"Bingo." He took a bite of his food. The buttery goodness of the flakey biscuit melted in his mouth. He hummed his appreciation.

"Thank you." She laughed before she asked, "Is he still that way?" She broke off a bit of her biscuit and popped it into her mouth.

He shook his head and swallowed hard. "See, that's just it, he isn't. It's like while I was gone, someone invaded Senior's body and took over. He's different now and it totally skews everything."

"Why do you think that is?" Gen asked as she took another bite.

"Honestly, I think it's because since I've been back, I don't give a shit whether or not he approves of me. Excuse the language."

"Excused. Kind of like a bully that stops picking on you when he realizes you can whop the crud out of him."

He took another bite and nodded. "Exactly like that." His mouth was full, but she got the gist of the answer.

They ate in silence for a minute or two before she jumped a bit. "Oh, Phil Granger is thinking about hiring someone to help out."

"Pumping gas?"

"He wants a mechanic, but he's willing to train them." She shrugged. "If I didn't like cooking so much, I'd jump on the job."

He snorted. "A mechanic?"

She narrowed her eyes at him. "You don't think I could do it?"

He held up his hands in surrender. "I think you could do anything you set your mind to, but the question would be why would you *want* to be a mechanic?"

She shrugged and laughed. "Just to see if I could.

KRIS MICHAELS

Oh, and as a side benefit, it would give Edna Michaelson something to be in a flutter over. She's still trying to find out what happened out at the Marshall Ranch."

"Something else will come along for her to wag her tongue over."

"Without a doubt." Gen finished her biscuit at the same time the timer for the oven went off. "That's my cue." She stood up and looked down at him. "Will I see you tonight for dinner?"

Andrew looked down at his coffee, "It's Friday night. Some would consider that a date."

Gen sat back down, and he glanced at her. She put her finger under his chin and turned his head so he was looking straight at her. "Andrew Hollister, this is me asking you out. I'm cooking dinner for you. It *is* a date."

"I'll be here." God help him, it would probably lead to disappointment for her and frustration for himself, but he fucking wanted to be *with* this woman. At least he knew he could make her feel good, even if it might not ever happen for him. His damn cock woke up at that thought. *Fucking hell.*

She leaned forward; her eyes traveled from his eyes to his lips. He didn't move, frozen in anticipation and afraid if he moved, she'd change her mind, yet she initiated the contact. The kiss was soft and sweet and held so much promise. He opened his eyes as she withdrew. "I'll see you later." She winked at him and stood; her hand trailed across his shoulders as she walked past him to the kitchen. His cock, awake and interested, made itself known. He grabbed his cowboy hat and slammed it onto his head. He had a date.

CHAPTER 6

Gen raced up the back stairs as soon as she finished cleaning. She'd been floating on excitement and anticipation all day. As soon as she was in the door, her t-shirt was off and she power-walked into her bedroom. She hadn't dressed up in eons. The last time was for a date in Rapid, a pediatrician she'd met through Eden and her son Jay. They'd dated for a couple months, but honestly, there was no chemistry, and sex was... meh, at best.

She shimmied out of her jeans and panties, flung them and her bra at the hamper, and jumped into the shower. The food for dinner tonight was downstairs. Did she add special touches to it that the regulars at the diner didn't get? Hell, yeah. Andrew had been stopping in for two weeks before the rest of the town woke up. The first week she'd tried to keep her hopes down, but when he kept showing up and they'd gotten to know each other, she hadn't been able to contain her excitement. Had she asked him out? Yep, because she'd probably be old and grey before he would make the move. Something was holding him back, but she didn't have that problem. She wanted to see where her intense attraction to this man would take them. God, she prayed he was attracted to her, too.

Her head buzzed and she stopped, taking several long deep breaths. *Settle down. This is a date. You've dated before. You can do this.* She washed and conditioned her hair, taking time to blow it dry straight and leaving it down around her shoulders. Bending down to the cupboard under the sink, she pushed her hairspray and lotion bottles out of the way. There. Her makeup.

She opened the bag and took inventory. Blush, a small tube of concealer, mascara that she hadn't opened. The powder blush had broken, but she could still use it. She opened her foundation and tipped it over. Whatever was in there had hardened to a rock. It wasn't coming out. She chucked the bottle and cap and fished around with her fingers to the bottom of the bag. They curled around a round tube. She pulled it out of the little bag. Lip gloss. Well… She looked at herself in the mirror. Mascara, blush, and lip gloss would have to do.

She carefully wiggled the mascara brush from the root of her lashes to the tip. Her eyes watered and her nose tingled. *No, don't sneeze. Don't…* Her eyes slammed shut and she sneezed three times. Gen slowly opened her eyes. *Crap on a cracker!* Mascara smudged on her cheek and up by her eyebrow.

She sighed, tied her hair back, and moved to the sink to wash her face. Staring at herself in the mirror, she chastised the reflection. "You really need to settle down, girl."

Finally, after successfully putting on her makeup and not sneezing herself into raccoon status again, she moved to her closet. She had jeans, good jeans and work jeans. There were three sundresses shoved in the back of the wardrobe, but that wasn't her any longer. She grabbed her best pair of jeans, designer label denim that cost way too much but made her ass look fantastic. A nice, cowl neck, sleeveless shirt, and a pair of dress boots. She spun in front of the full-length mirror. "You'll do."

She was trotting down the stairs when Andrew's truck pulled up behind her diner. She stopped at the bottom of the stairs, and he got out of the truck. He smiled and flicked his gaze over her. "You look amazing."

She stepped closer to him. "Right back at you, cowboy." His shirt was crisply pressed, and he wore expensive boots that were alligator or maybe ostrich. God, he looked better than good, and the fact he made a point of dressing up too made her giddy. "I was just going to grab our dinner." She motioned to the back of the diner.

"Need a hand?"

"As a matter of fact, yes," she admitted. Drew fell into step with her. "I should have had this done before you got here."

"We didn't say a time…" His sentence trailed away.

"Well, I'm glad you're here. If I had to wait, I'd be a bigger ball of nerves." She opened the door, and he held it for her so she could go in.

"Why would you be nervous?"

She turned around so she could see him and laughed. "Because it has been at least ten million years since I've been on a date."

"Only ten million?"

"Yep." She spun again and walked across the kitchen toward the warming drawer where their dinner waited.

A loud banging at her front door stopped her in her tracks. "Want me to get that?" Andrew's brow creased.

"Yes, if you would." Everyone in town knew to come to her apartment if they needed something after she'd closed. She turned off the oven and grabbed a set of potholders. The banging started up again. *What in the heck? Was someone dying?* Gen put the potholders she'd grabbed down and headed into the front of the diner. "Drew? Who in the world is banging on the door?"

Andrew did a double-take at the man pounding on the door. He opened it just as the man started to pound again. Andrew looked down and assessed the person in front of him. His tailored suit and shiny, pointy-toed leather shoes were designer brands. His orange-tinted spray tan was just as out of place as his too-blonde hair which looked like it had been styled with hairspray. The man reached up and flicked something off his suit jacket. "Genevieve Wheeler, please?"

"Drew? Who in the world is banging on the door?" Gen walked around the corner and stopped short. "What? Ah... why? I mean... how?" She shook her head as if she needed to reboot her brain after seeing the man at the door. "No. What are you doing here?"

The Oompa Loompa-looking man glanced at and dismissed Andrew with an offhanded huff and walked to the counter. "Genevieve, may I speak with you, please?"

Andrew left the door open and followed the offensive little man into the diner. The color had drained from Gen's face and her easy, ready smile vanished. She stepped to the left, away from the suited shithead and closer to where Andrew was standing. She blinked and shook her head. "No. No, that's not going to happen. You need to go back from wherever you sprouted from. How in the world did you get here?"

"What do you mean, no? I came all this way to discuss rectifying what happened. It was a horrid journey and I'm exhausted." The man once again flicked an invisible piece of something from his suit jacket.

She seemed to snap out of whatever shock she'd been caught in. "No. Not only no, but hell, no. I don't want to talk with you, to you, or about you. You should leave. Now. Seriously."

A haggard sigh fell from the man. "Gen, please, may we speak in private? Let me explain to you what happened." His words were smooth, and they held a calculated quality that set every nerve Andrew had on edge. The man fell firmly into snake oil salesman category. Andrew moved and casually rounded the two of them to stand between them. Whoever this was, the two of them had a history, and based on the signs Gen was throwing, it wasn't a pleasant one, either. He'd watched Gen for weeks now. He'd been a recipient of her charm and hospitality. What he was seeing now was another side of her personality, and her reaction to Mr. Oompa brought every ounce of protective testosterone in his body to the forefront. Drew's hand tightened into a fist as he reminded himself that this wasn't his place and she hadn't asked him to step in. Yet. *Fuck, ask me, Gen, hell, just look this way, and I'm so up in this man's shit.*

Gen stepped forward so she was standing next to him, stopping within inches of his shoulder. He could feel her warmth and her agitation. She laughed. A deep, bitter sound expelled before she shook her head and sighed, "*Explain?* What could you possibly say?" She snapped her fingers and jumped a bit. "Oh! Wait! I know! Chelsea had a gun to your head and you *had* to screw her? No, wait that couldn't be right, could it? What with her on all fours and you ramming her from behind, that would be next to impossible, wouldn't it? How about you were tempted beyond your resistance? Oh, I know… you were drugged, right?"

Gears locked into place. The ex. Drew crossed his arms over his chest and smirked. Gen was just getting spun up. He couldn't wait to hear what she had to say to the asshole. Gen stepped forward and pointed at the man, "You were supposed to be at work. You took her to my apartment! *My* apartment! You were having an affair *for months* with my best friend!" Gen turned and looked at Andrew. "Can I shoot him?"

"Technically, no. We opened the door. Castle doctrine doesn't apply now." He shrugged.

"Damn it." She turned back to the man who stood with a perplexed look on his face. "Really, Avery, there is nothing you can say that would even remotely make me want to be in the same room with you. You need to leave. Seriously, you're wasting my time. I have a date, so if you don't mind…"

"Now, Genevieve, your mother said—"

Andrew winced. Even after only two weeks, he knew Gen's mom was a hot-button topic. This guy was clueless. Gen lifted her arm and pointed to the door. "Get out before I call the sheriff and have you arrested for trespassing."

Andrew's eyes bounced from Gen to the orange asshat. Amazingly, the man chuckled. "Now, honey, your mom said you would be upset. I know I made a mistake or perhaps an error in judgment, but it's over between Chelsea and me. That was a mistake. No big deal. Now, for the love of God, go get your purse and lock the doors on this hovel, it is time for you to grow up and come back home. You ran away when the going got tough. Please stop being so emotional and let's go talk." The man spoke to her as if she was a petulant child and then he made his first and last mistake. He grabbed Gen's arm.

Andrew was at the end of his rope with this son of a bitch. He stepped forward, his six-foot-seven frame dwarfing the man in front of him. Taking the man's forearm in his grip, he squeezed until the bastard let go of Gen. He moved again, completely blocking Genevieve from the stranger's view. "Mister, it looks to me like you are good at making mistakes. I do believe the lady asked you to leave. You can do that one of two ways, on your feet or on your ass." He issued the threat as if he was commenting on the weather, but the look he gave the man was all business.

"Now see here, this is between Genevieve and me. You have absolutely no right to insert yourself into this conversation." If the ex's indignation wasn't so absolute it would have been comical.

Andrew shook his head. Mr. Oompa was going to have to learn things the hard way. "Wrong answer, little man. I have every right, unlike you." He cupped the man's shoulder and spun him around, grabbing the expensive shirt collar and beltline of the shocked idiot. Andrew lifted him off the ground, immediately sending the man's arms and legs splaying. A string of cuss words sounded from the front of the suit.

Andrew nodded at Genevieve. "Would you mind holding that door open so I can take out the trash?"

Genevieve ran to the door and grabbed the handle, keeping it open. Andrew took three steps and heaved his load forward with the same motion he'd perfected pitching bales of hay. Avery flew out the door, past the sidewalk, and into the street, landing in a heap. People on the street froze as Andrew walked onto the sidewalk after the flying man. The noise and business of the small town on a Friday afternoon stopped as if suspended in time. Andrew didn't care that he was now the center of attention. "Little man, this is *my* town. These are *my* people. She asked you to leave. Leave. Now."

Avery stood and looked at the blood from the road rash burn on his hands. He made a dramatic gesture down to his now ruined slacks. "Who the fuck do you think you are? I am going to have you arrested for assault! Do you know how much this suit cost?"

Drew chuffed out a laugh. "Arrested? Find a witness, you idiot. You tripped." Andrew nodded toward Doc Macy, who was standing across the street. "Doc, did you see anyone assault this man?"

Doc shook his head and raised his voice so everyone could hear him, "Saw him trip over his own feet and land face down in the street. Has he been drinking? Should I call the sheriff and have a sobriety test done on him? He could be endangering our young ones if he is drinking and driving this early."

Phillip Granger walked over from his garage. "Darnedest thing, Andrew, I saw that man fall flat on his face when he walked off that curb."

Avery's face twisted with rage. He looked at Genevieve, "You are seriously going to stand there and allow this to happen?"

She shrugged. "You really should watch where you walk, Avery. It's been a blast. Don't come back."

At her slowly spreading smile, Avery lost all remnants of his composure. "You are obviously not worth the time or effort I've invested in you. You're such a pathetically cold bitch. Why do you think I screwed around on you? Making love to you is like making love to a dead fish. I had to find good sex with someone else. God knows you could *never* satisfy anyone. You'll never find anyone who will put up with you. I am your only chance!"

Andrew's fists clenched. He jolted toward the smaller man. His chest rumbled with a growl of rage. Avery pawed open his car door, dove into the vehicle, and locked it. Andrew slammed his hand on the hood, denting it. The asshole jammed his car into reverse and then tore down 1st Street as fast as his electric hybrid would carry him.

Andrew turned and nodded to Doc and Phil. He drew a breath and glanced up and down the street. Edna Michaelson stood with her mouth open at the door of Sanderson's Market. *Wonderful. Just what Gen needed.* He rolled his shoulders and turned toward her. "Let's get back inside."

Gen jumped a bit and looked up at him. "Yeah, good idea. I think I'll be the next topic for the town gossip mongers." Gen waved at Mrs. Michaelson. He waited for Genevieve to move inside so he could shut the door. She walked to the first counter stool where she quietly sat down. Her body trembled, and tears ran down her cheeks.

"You shouldn't be upset. He's gone."

Her head jerked up. "Upset? God, no. I'm pissed!" She swiped away her tears. "I cry when I'm really mad. I hate it, but I do. The audacity of that bastard." She looked at her hand. "And now I'm a raccoon again."

Andrew handed her a napkin from one of the dispensers. "He was something. I'll give you that. Thought you two were long done."

She threw up her hands. "See, that's the thing, we are." She blinked and shook her head. "*Years* done, and he shows up out of the blue." She stopped and then looked at him. "My mother had something to do with this. Damn it, I knew she was up to something."

"I have no idea what you're talking about, but I

think we both need a drink. Do you have anything upstairs?"

She shook her head. "No, but if I am going to be the center of Edna Michaelson's gossip of the month club, a drink sounds wonderful. I mean, the entire town knows far too much about me right now."

"They *know* you and they *don't* know him. Who do you think they are going to side with? Him? No. He lost that war when he drove into town in that electric car."

Gen snorted out a laugh. "God, what a first date. Can I die of embarrassment?"

Andrew walked over and squatted in front of her so they were face to face. "Nobody has ever died of embarrassment. That's a proven medical fact."

She chuckled. "Did you Google that?"

He nodded. "A long time ago, and I can guarantee ninety-nine percent of this town, me included, have had their lives dissected by the gossips and cronies that feed on that crap. We survived, and I promise you will, too."

"I can't believe I thought that I loved him. What kind of glasses was I wearing? He is such an asshat."

Andrew chuckled. "Yeah, he was a work of art." Orange-tinted, ass-encrusted art. He stood and looked down at her. "Let's go to The Bit and Spur and have a few drinks."

She nodded and stood up. "That sounds like an

awesome plan. I need to take the food upstairs first and fix my makeup. Could you lock that door?"

"On it." He locked the door, turned off the light, and followed Gen back to the kitchen. "If he comes back, I'd like to know."

She chuckled. "After you literally tossed him out of here? I really don't think that's likely to happen. He is a lot of things, but perpetually stupid? Not so much."

CHAPTER 7

Andrew looked out the picture window of Gen's apartment. The town was closing down for the day. He watched Phil close and lock the garage door and smiled as he walked toward The Bit and Spur. Like clockwork. Maggie Patterson laughed and waved to someone in Sanderson's Market as she left with a small bag of goods. Most everyone made monthly trips to one of the bigger towns to lay in supplies, but the Sandersons stocked items that people tended to run out of. He could hear Gen moving around in the apartment. He watched as Carson Schmidt's truck drove from behind the hardware store and headed to his home about three miles away. The little town didn't change. He found a unique sense of safety in that fact. Rather like his father's ranch. Hands came and went, but the ranch was a constant. He glanced at his watch. And if it wasn't for his interest in Gen, he'd be there now working with Smokey and her new colt or checking on the herd.

Andrew rolled his shoulders and put his hands on his hips as he stared sightlessly out of the picture window. Of all the seriously jacked-up paths he could have taken to get here, back in South Dakota. He was going to make the Marines his life. Then his RECON squad had walked into a staged IED and an ambush. Intelligence for the area they were patrolling was normally considered tainted, but the intel on that day... it was fucked. The IED had killed all but three of his men. An insurgent force had surrounded his RECON team and pinned them down. He and Gunny had fought for almost twenty-four hours until ground forces could reach them. Twenty-four hours of pure, unadulterated hell. Jose was medically retired, the FNG —or Fucking New Guy—was mangled from the explosion and mentally torn to shreds. His body recovered, but his mind... well, they told him the kid didn't fare as well. And Pip had suffered major shrapnel wounds and died three days after they helicoptered him out.

Andrew had survived the blast but also suffered injuries. The vivid scars that no one but his doctors had seen criss crossed his lower abdomen, thighs, and groin. According to the Corps, his physical injuries were repaired. *Yeah, right.*

The shrinks the Marines had forced him to talk with and the medical docs had finally agreed on a diagnosis which led to his discharge. After seven months of rehab and therapy, they'd cut him loose and written him off. What did it matter that his body didn't function? Who the fuck cared if his mind was shattered by recurring images of the devastation and horror that had happened? He drifted through the thoughts as he watched the people move along the quiet street. Hell, the head shrink had said it was possible Andrew would never again experience sex with a woman. Physically, the doctors had said he should be capable, but the almost-debilitating apathy that had consumed him since the attack had denied him any physical reaction around a woman… until Genevieve smiled at him that morning he'd first arrived at her diner. The painful flood of blood to his lower regions when she smiled at him that morning shocked him to his core. He'd fled the diner, running away from her and the reaction she'd caused. He was such a chickenshit. If he could have kicked himself, he would have gladly, often, and hard.

Gen's open and friendly presence floored him, and he had no concept of how to deal with the physical reaction of his body. Well, that was bullshit. He *did* know what to do, and this afternoon, he'd reached climax while thinking about her in the shower. And didn't that make him feel like a letch? The fact that his thoughts hadn't wandered to his team or what happened that day was a freaking miracle.

Shit, maybe that was why he turned up at her doorstep the next day… and the one after that. When he was with her, he wasn't there. Even working on the ranch, his mind constantly traveled back to that day. With Gen, it was as if his mind was able to find shelter from the storm of his past.

And, if he was honest, he wanted to make sure his reactions weren't some kind of a fluke. God, they so weren't. His body reacted to that sexy woman. And sweet baby Jesus, the how's and why's didn't matter. The simple fact was that she mattered.

Mattered enough that when her ex showed up, he was ready to go caveman. She'd said this morning she wanted there to be some reason other than her cooking for him to keep coming into her diner. God, there was a myriad of reasons. But how in the hell did he tell her, and did she even want to know?

The glorified city pansy had spoken to her like a spoiled child, and that had pissed him off. Anger had slammed through him. Instinctual, base, and feral, he'd seethed as he grabbed the little man and threw him from the diner. Andrew had managed to stop on the sidewalk, but how, he didn't have a clue. He'd wanted nothing more than to pound the shit out of the manicured puff of a man, especially after the comments he'd screamed at Genevieve in front of half the residents of Hollister.

His mind snapped back to the present as his eyes lingered on the vacant sidewalk across the street. The corners of his lips lifted slightly as he felt his body stir at the thought of her. She had been wearing skintight jeans, high-heeled boots, and a white, silky top that hugged every curve. The seductive sway of her hips and outline of her fantastic body had grabbed his attention like a big mouth bass striking after a shiny lure. He wanted to chase that sparkle. *Yeah, you've hooked me hard, sweetheart.*

"Are you ready to go?" Gen walked into her front room.

"I am. You do know the Bit can get active and a bit rough on a Friday night, right?"

"Boy howdy, do I. My brother Jeremiah came into town and broke up a knife fight between Declan and two guys. He knocked the drunks out but not before they knifed Declan. Jeremiah kept Declan from pulling the knife out until Eden and Zeke got there."

Andrew narrowed his eyes. "When was that?"

"Oh, when Jeremiah first came to town." Gen smiled and pointed toward the back door. "Drinks and then back here to eat?"

"Sounds like a plan." He escorted her out of the apartment and down the stairs.

"Walk or drive?" Gen asked as they approached his truck.

"Walk." They wandered down the alley behind the hardware store and headed toward the bar. "So, growing up here, you know everyone, huh?"

"Everyone except the newcomers." He nodded. He'd gone to school with most of them.

"And *we* think of *you* as a newcomer. Funny how that is, isn't it?" She chuckled. "I love this little town."

"It has its charms." Her being the only one he could think of at the moment. He rolled his eyes at himself. He pulled open the door to the bar and looked over at her. "What's your drink?"

"Tonight? Whiskey."

"Grab a booth and I'll get the drinks." Gen smiled and headed to the back of the bar. He didn't want her with him when he talked to Declan. They had a history. Well, the truth be told, Andrew had a history with Declan's sister, one that had ended long after it should have.

"Hollister." Declan purposefully turned his attention to Gen. "You staking a new claim?"

"Your sister is ancient history. She needs to stay there."

"Did I say anything?" The man growled the words.

"No, and you won't, and because I respect you, I won't, either. Whiskey. A bottle, please."

"She's never been in here with anyone before. Seems you cracked the ice princess' shell." Declan grabbed two glasses and a bottle of Jameson.

Andrew gave the man behind the bar a withering glance. "She has had a really bad day, Declan. And what she does and who she does it with is none of your business. Give me the damn glasses."

Declan handed him two glasses and the bottle and turned back to the bar to finish stocking the beer cooler. Andrew walked across the dance floor and set the empty glasses on the table at the booth where she sat. He licked his fingers and stretched over the table, unscrewing the light in the sconce above the table, draping the corner in darkness. Relaxing into the booth, he rested his back against the wall, and he reached for the bottle, pouring a shot of the amber liquid into his glass.

Genevieve looked across the table at him. "Funny, I don't think that was a happy conversation. Between you and Declan, I mean."

He sipped the whiskey and shrugged. "When you grow up in a small town, you have a history. It happens."

Genevieve squinted her eyes at him as she leaned back against the wall and stretched her legs out over the bench seat as he had done. "I'm going to apologize in advance. I may not be good company tonight. Which sucks because I really wanted tonight to be amazing."

Andrew rolled his head against the wall and looked at her. "Obviously, the town grapevine isn't working. If it was, you would know that I'm never good company."

Genevieve laughed, finished her drink, and poured herself another one. She waited for Andrew to finish his and poured him one, too. "That's a lie. All those morning conversations have proved otherwise. But can I ask you a question?"

"Sure, what is it?" He watched the door open and two cowboys come in and belly up to the bar.

"Why do you avoid coming into town?"

He looked over at her. She was running her finger around the rim of her glass, not looking at him, which made it a bit easier to answer. "Because not a lot of what happens here is important."

She looked up at him, and her brows curled together in confusion.

He shifted on the bench, still sprawled across the seat but looking more at her. "Most of the time, my thoughts are back in that country. I'm stuck in that day and the events." He lifted his glass and stared into the honey-brown liquid. "Everything was life and death. For twenty-four hours, every move I made, everything I thought or did, could cost another life. Being around people after that seemed…" He shrugged. He didn't have the words for the emptiness and uselessness he felt.

"Empty, almost fake, like what is important to them isn't even a blip on your screen," Gen finished for him.

He snapped his gaze up to meet hers. "Exactly."

She nodded. "That's what Jeremiah told me he felt like after he witnessed that serial killer torture two people he knew. He's been through hell, too." She downed her whiskey and poured herself another one.

"Hell. Yeah, I had a first-class ticket." Andrew gulped his drink down and extended his glass. She splashed another finger's worth of liquor into the glass and leaned back against the wall. She needed this. A chance to decompress and think about what had happened today. All of what had happened, with both Andrew and Avery.

Genevieve glanced at him through her lashes, trying to figure him out. His physical presence seemed so intense that the air thinned, almost as if it were sucked out of the space he inhabited. He had a resting bitch face that probably scared most everyone away. The deep furrows in his brow and the hard, searching gazes could make people uncomfortable. Yet she wasn't put off by his demeanor. His quietness could be mistaken for aloofness, and originally, she would have made that assumption, but the man sitting across from her was more than the sum of what she saw. He was putting up a shield, one he didn't let many people see behind. It didn't hurt that his larger-than-life presence overshadowed everyone, especially her pissant ex-fiancé, Avery. No doubt about it, the fierce, hulking man was gorgeous.

She sipped her whiskey and replayed this afternoon's incident once again. Seeing Avery so unexpectedly had shocked her. Her outburst when he stated he wanted to talk to her came from nothing but long-ago forgotten but obviously bottled-up hurt and anger. She felt the heat in her face again as she remembered the way she dumped all her dirty laundry in front of Andrew Hollister. God, she was mortified, but her shock and disbelief had been automatic.

The things that Avery had done had hurt her deeply. She closed her eyes and recounted his rant from the street. Could she really be to blame for his cheating? Granted, sex with him had never been great, nothing like the earth-shattering sex she read about in the romance novels she loved. But she knew *he* got off, and she'd believed his needs were satisfied even though she knew hers weren't.

Avery had been considered a prize because of his successful career, his connections, and the fact that he was an heir to a fortune. Avery was everything she was raised to believe she wanted in a husband. Her mom loved him, and her dad tolerated him. Avery acted like he loved her, but in hindsight, she wondered if he wanted to marry her just to get closer to her father's substantial political influence. Her father was an extremely wealthy, very influential man, and he could be a powerful person with whom to be aligned.

Gen sipped at her drink. The first three shots were doing their job. Her embarrassment over Avery's appearance was something she could sweep away. They sat in a comfortable silence, watching the patrons of the bar arrive while slowly sipping their whiskey. She felt no need to talk, his quiet presence warm and reassuring. She knew no one would dare invade his space, and by association, she felt protected, sitting with him in the booth.

The minutes ticked by and turned into hours, and still, they sat. Conversation ebbed and flowed naturally. The comfort she felt tucked into the back booth in the dark bar shouldn't have been this soothing, but it was.

Gen felt that wonderful numbness all around the edges. And that lack of feeling? Oh, man, it kinda rocked.

As the bar crowd filled in, Declan turned up the country music, cranking the volume so individual conversations could not be easily distinguished. Several men from surrounding ranches and the livestock yard stood at the bar and cast curious looks at the table she and Andrew occupied. Oh yeah, no doubt in her mind they had heard what had happened at the diner. In reality, the morbid embarrassment caused by Avery's disgusting accusations stung. Stung? Hell, it hurt like a bitch. Looking over at her very quiet drinking partner, she cleared her throat and asked, "Hey... do I look like a cold fish to you?"

Andrew turned his head toward her and scanned her body with intense, brown eyes, "Nope." He nodded toward the bar. "Every man at that bar wants to date you, by the way. I don't think any of them would date a cold fish."

Gen whipped her head toward him. "Really? How do you know they wouldn't date a fish?"

The ridiculousness of her comment must have stunned him, and when she started laughing, he joined in. Genevieve reached across the table, putting her hand on his arm. "No, no, no... that didn't come out right. Stop laughing at me, Andrew! Really, what I meant was... how do you know they want to date me, not that they wouldn't date a cold fish?"

Andrew sat up in the booth and faced her, not moving the arm she held. He poured them both another drink. "When Declan and I spoke earlier, he asked if I was staking my claim on you. He basically said you'd turned down everyone. Besides, I don't date fish."

Genevieve laughed so hard she snorted, causing him to laugh at her again. The looks from the men at the bar were overt and lingered this time. She shook his arm with her hand as she bounced up and down on the booth seat across from him, laughing like an excited child. Whatever, the liquor made her act like a loon, she'd deal with it tomorrow. She leaned across the table and stage whispered, "What do y'all think I am… a mound of dirt? Staking a claim. That's so caveman." She snorted at her own joke, which made her laugh harder and snort again. She slapped a hand over her face and dissolved into uncontrollable giggles. The regulars at the bar smiled as they looked her way. She reached across the table and possessively put both hands on Andrew's arm.

Andrew smiled and shook his head as he attempted to sip his drink. He crooked his finger at her, and she leaned further across the table. She waited, wide-eyed and smiling as his deep voice rolled over her. "No, you are a very sexy woman who needs to dance with me."

Gen blinked at him, his words shocking her. She leaned closer, and in a stage whisper, asked, "Seriously, you think I'm sexy?"

When his smile faded and he nodded his head, she cocked hers "And exactly why should I dance with you, sir? Have you staked your claim?"

Andrew stood and held out his hand to her. "Yes, woman, I have. Do you have a problem with that?"

She put her hand in his and stood up, swaying from the lack of food and heavy doses of alcohol. He put his arm around her, and she leaned into him, putting her arms on his massive biceps, feeling the steel of the man that held her. Her body heated, and she had drunk enough to enjoy the sensations running through her without feeling any qualms about letting him know it. "Ummm… no, I can honestly say I don't have a problem with that. Absolutely none at all. I may when I become sober, but at the moment… I think I liked being staked or claimed or whatever it was you said."

He led off, putting his leg between hers and pulling her tightly against him. The feel of his thigh between her legs sent a warm flood drenching her panties, and she pushed against the hard muscles of his thigh, loving the sensation. His magnificent body smelled like the outdoors, clean and fresh. She laid her head on his shoulder and breathed deeply. He chuckled, "I believe you are the tallest woman I have ever danced with."

She smiled and lifted her head, looking up into his eyes. His dark brown eyes were hooded and sexy. "I love wearing these boots. Avery would never let me. He said it made me too tall and made everyone else uncomfortable."

Andrew stopped in the middle of the floor and looked at her. "I like you in heels. It's sexy as hell and a massive turn-on. I could give a shit less what other people think."

He started dancing again, and she fell into step with him. His hand traveled up her back, and he held her neck under her hair. He cradled her as they danced. Gen lost herself in the feel of his body and the sound of the music. Andrew sighed, "God, you smell good, like springtime."

She smiled, enjoying the feel of him so close to her. The music switched to a country anthem that brought more people to the dancefloor. He stopped and held her. A shiver of desire rippled through her body. He kissed her cheek lightly and walked her back to the booth. Andrew held her hand and sat down in the booth, pulling her in after him. Leaning back against the wall, he pulled her back into his chest as they sat, looking out into the bar that had filled to capacity. He poured them both a drink, and she rested her arm on his knee he had lifted onto the seat. She swirled the brown liquid as the people pretended not to watch them.

Gen's alcohol-and-sex-addled brain suddenly clicked with a clear thought. She turned her head toward him. "You do realize, of course, our dancing and me sitting like this is going to cause quite the gossip session. Edna will have a field day."

When he laughed, the rumbling of his chest

vibrated through her. "Am I to assume that bothers you?"

She took another drink and laid her head back onto his chest, shaking her head slowly. "Nope. If you're good with it, I am, too."

He mindlessly twirled her hair in his fingers. "See that guy in the green shirt at the end of the bar?"

She turned her head, looking at the man, and nodded. "Yep, I know him. That's Zeke Johnson."

Andrew lowered his lips to her ear and whispered, "He just broke up with his girlfriend in Buffalo."

She lifted her eyes toward him. "No way! How do you know that?"

He laughed, "Ranch hands. Damn men cluck like chickens about who is doing what with whom and who wants to do who."

Genevieve's hand slid over his thigh as he nuzzled her neck and ear, gently nibbling on both. She drew a deep breath as his hand traveled up her leg and hovered over her hot, wet core.

The moment dissolved partially when a disturbance at the bar pulled their attention toward the front of the establishment. Four women that Gen had never seen before had walked in and immediately elevated the noise level of the bar. She groaned. "Great, freaking woo-hoo girls."

Andrew stopped playing with her hair for a moment. His hand still rested between her legs. "Woo-hoo girls?"

She nodded and spoke, trying hard to enunciate each word. She may have had a titch too much whiskey tonight. "Just watch as soon as someone buys them a drink. Ten bucks says they shout, 'Woo-hoo,' and either chug or shoot the drink."

"Really?"

His comment was said into her hair. He couldn't have been looking at the women, but Gen felt it her obligation to warn him about the dangers of woo-hoo girls. "Yep. Then, after a sufficient amount of alcohol has been consumed, they will case the joint, figure out who they want to go home with, and start the hunt." She'd seen the stalk-and-hunt tactic too many times to count at local bars when she was going to Brown.

She held her glass out for Andrew to refill because why not. She was celebrating… or forgetting. *No, she was celebrating forgetting.* Yep. That was it. Gen shook her head and lifted her newly refilled glass. "Be afraid, gentlemen, be very afraid. Woo-hoo girls are lethal, deadly animals."

He laughed and refilled his glass. "Lethal-deadly? That is rather redundant, isn't it? Besides, I have you to protect me from the badass woo-hoo girls, don't I?"

Gen giggled. "Doubly redundant. My professors at Brown would not approve. But don't worry, Andrew, I'll protect you."

He pulled her hair gently. "Drew. Just Drew."

She looked at him and smiled before she pointed to the whiskey. One of them would have to move to recover it, and she was very happy exactly where she was. "Well, Drew, what are we going to do about a very, very perplexing situation we have on our hands?" She gave him her best librarian look but wasn't quite sure she'd hit the mark when he laughed at her. They needed to get some food, or they'd be hurting in the morning.

"I can think of several perplexing situations we have on our hands, Gen. May I ask which one you are talking about?" He put his arm around her waist and pulled her back, closer to his body. She knew his situation immediately when she felt his hard desire against her lower back.

"Oh, I like your situation better. Let's talk about that one." Whether the alcohol, the darkness of the corner, or the attraction she felt toward him lowered her inhibitions, she couldn't say. Okay, she could; it was the alcohol that emboldened her to do something she never would have dreamed of doing before tonight. Gen deftly rotated her hips back against his body and ran her hand farther up his thigh. His deep groan rumbled through his chest behind her. She shifted and looked back at him. The desire in his eyes echoed hers. She licked her lips and dropped her eyes to his sensual mouth. God, he was magnificent.

"Gen, we are both pretty tanked, you really should stop." She pulled her eyes to his and looked at his lips and then back to his eyes. A very deep, low growl of desire emanated from him as he lowered his lips to hers. Her tongue licked his lips, and she sucked his bottom lip into her mouth. He pulled away and looked at her. "I think I should take you home."

She blinked and looked at him blankly for a moment until what he suggested clicked. That was a great idea. She smiled and swiveled her hips into his hard cock once again to let him know she agreed with his line of thought. "Okay, cowboy, I think you should take me home, too."

He had started to move her out in front of him and then pulled her to a sudden stop. "Gen, I am going to take you home to put you to bed... I mean, to sleep. So you won't regret your actions in the morning."

She contorted her body so she could see him and licked her lips and then bit the bottom one. "Mmmm... all right, Drew, take me home and put me in my bed." She purred, "I promise neither you nor I will sleep or regret our actions in the morning."

He pushed her again, gently moving her out of the booth, pausing to pull his wallet out. He retrieved a handful of bills to throw onto the table and held her hand as they walked across the dance floor. One of the girls Gen had pointed out earlier walked up to Drew and put her hand on his arm, stopping him. "Hey, handsome, why don't *you* buy *me* a drink?" Gen watched as Drew paused and looked down at the woman.

Oh, hell, no, Gen wasn't going to let a woman wearing rodeo clown makeup touch her man. She stepped back and positioned herself between Drew and the trespasser. Gen put her hand on his cheek and smiled at him, leaning up to kiss him. Her tongue tentatively sought his. He wrapped his huge, muscled arms around her body and pulled her close. He immediately deepened his kiss, claiming her mouth. When he finally pulled away from her, both were breathless from the kiss. Damn, the man was perfection. He smiled down at her as she ran her finger over his bottom lip.

Gen lifted an eyebrow and looked over at the shocked little woman still standing next to them. She knew as her blood alcohol level increased so did her Southern accent, but Gen deliberately laid it on thick and drawled with her best Alabama twang, "Honey child, y'all want to back the hell on up now? This man is *so* taken."

CHAPTER 8

Drew looked directly at Declan, knowing for a fact the man had heard Gen's comment. The history between them should have concerned him, but he'd be damned if his past was going to fuck up this. Stephanie had no part in his present, and Declan needed to understand that. The bartender's glare sent a look of hatred. He was beyond caring how Declan justified slapping him with the responsibility for Stephanie. He hadn't done anything wrong.

Drew took Gen's hand and pulled her from the bar behind him. Gen looked back at the little blonde as Drew pulled her through the crowd and smiled as she yelled back, taunting, "Y'all have a good night now, darlin'. Ya hear? Bless your sweet little heart."

He put his arm around her shoulders and pulled her tight against him as they left the busy bar. He led her past the trucks parked in the pea gravel and headed toward the sidewalk. "You do realize what you just did, right?"

She hummed and nudged him with her hip. "Ummm, let me see if my alcohol-addled mind can recall my actions. We drank *a lot* of whiskey."

Her accent had become more pronounced as the evening had advanced, and her Southern drawl was sexy as hell. He nodded, affirming her truth. "Yes, we did, but after that."

She lifted her eyes toward the sky. "Umm... I figured out y'all kinda like me."

He chuckled, "Not going to deny it. After that."

"I kissed you, and you, sir... kissed me back. I particularly like that part." She put her hand in his back pocket as they walked around the corner and started down the block toward her diner.

"Yeah, me too, but I mean after that."

She held up her fingers and ran through the events and then hopped up and down, "Oh! I told that bleached-blonde bimbo of a bitch that you were taken. Ohhh... wow! Do *you* have a problem with that?"

He looked both ways and then stepped off the side-walk, heading toward her diner. "Absolutely not, I think I like being staked or claimed or whatever it was you did back there."

She smiled at him as they stepped up onto the side-walk. He pulled her into his arms and lowered his lips to hers. Her arms wrapped around his neck, and he fisted her long, thick hair, pulling her head back, giving him access to her throat and jaw. He nibbled along her jaw and kissed her neck as her hands dropped and explored the muscles of his chest and shoulders. He was suddenly glad for all the hard work that left him ripped.

"You fucking bitch!" The venomous voice that came from the street in front of her diner startled them. Gen spun in his arms. The fucking Oompa Loompa from this morning strode toward them, holding a baseball bat. "Are you screwing this ape? Do you think this hayseed can afford you? Get your ass in that car now and I may not beat the shit out of him."

Drew carefully moved Genevieve behind him. "Let me handle this."

"Okay. Hey, Drew? Just don't kill him, okay? I couldn't stand it if *you* had to go to jail tonight." The smile her comment caused disappeared as he turned to the approaching fool.

He measured the man who strode toward him. Andrew growled, "Bring it on, partner, but fair warning… that bat isn't going to be enough to take me out." Drew waited for Avery to make the first move and blocked the swinging bat with his left forearm. Drew's right hook launched as the bat struck and landed solidly, knocking the smaller man down to the pavement. The resounding thud of Avery's head hitting the ground would have been sickening if the bastard hadn't brought a bat to a fistfight.

Blue strobe lights flashed off the glass of the diner.

Drew lifted his eyes to the patrol car to see Ken walking toward them. His car had stopped in the middle of the street, and the emergency lights bounced off the buildings, shattering the darkness.

"Damn it, Andrew, that was one hell of a right hook." The deputy sheriff kicked the bat away from the unconscious man and felt for a pulse. "Well, you didn't kill him. If someone came after me and my woman with a bat, I probably wouldn't have stopped."

Drew nodded. "Yeah, well, if he hadn't broken my wrist with that bat, I would have thrown a follow-up punch."

"Damn it, Drew, that's nasty as hell." Ken reached for his radio. "You very well may need surgery. I wish Zeke was still in town."

Drew nodded toward the bar and winced as Gen moved his arm, looking at the break. "He was in The Bit and Spur about five minutes ago."

Ken radioed to dispatch to call the volunteer medics who manned the ambulance. "Roger that, Jackie, the unconscious man who attacked Mr. Hollister will need a doctor. Mr. Hollister also needs Zeke to take a look at his arm." He instructed them to call the bar to get Doc Johnson up to the clinic.

Drew put his good arm around Genevieve and pulled her closer. "It was self-defense, Ken." He wasn't going to jail. He could just imagine Senior's outrage.

Ken chuckled. "I saw the whole thing. The man took a homerun swing at you with that bat. You put one right hook on him, and he dropped like a ton of bricks. It was self-defense, plain and simple." Ken bent down and positioned the unconscious man. "I don't think he will, but I'm going to make sure he doesn't choke on the blood from the injuries. I'd bet this guy has a broken nose, maybe a possible broken jaw, and probably a concussion."

Doc Zeke ran around the corner and straight to the small crowd that had started to gather in front of the diner. "Gen, are you all right?"

"Yeah, Zeke, I am fine, it was Andrew that was attacked. Avery decided to take a baseball bat after Andrew, his last mistake today, I would think."

Drew squeezed Gen closer to him and nodded. She smiled at him and put her head on his shoulder and whispered, "Are you all right?"

He put his lips to her forehead and kissed her gently before he responded, "My wrist is killing me. To be completely honest, if I wasn't so drunk, I would be cussing a blue streak right now. I think I am going to be in some serious pain come morning."

She slid her hand from his shoulder to his chest. "And I was so looking forward to you putting me to bed tonight." His low growl and tightening grip let her know he had been looking forward to it, too.

A low wail could be heard in the distance, and more people started to congregate on the corner of East Main and First Street. Ken Zorn stood up and nodded toward Phillip Granger. "Get those fools out of the street and clear a path for the ambulance, will ya, Phil?"

"You got it, Ken." The older man's voice rang with authority, directing the onlookers to move back to the sidewalk.

After Zeke completed his exam, the ambulance attendants loaded Avery onto the stretcher and placed their charge into the back of the ambulance. Zeke herded Andrew toward the bus. "Come on, you need to have that put into an air splint. Once we get to the hospital, it is going to have to be set at a minimum, and surgery is a very real possibility."

Gen walked with him to the ambulance. Zeke shook his head. "Not enough room in the bus for all of us, Gen. You can drive to Rapid City tomorrow. This big lug needs to sober up, and if we need to do surgery, he is going to be there a couple days."

Drew pulled her close. "My keys are in my right front pocket. Bring my truck and come to Rapid tomorrow and pick me up?" She reached into his pocket and retrieved his keys.

She smiled up at him. "Rain check for tonight?"

He leaned down and kissed her. "Oh yeah, as long as it is redeemable at the earliest possible moment." She smiled and leaned up to kiss him again.

"All right, you two, we really do have to go." Zeke opened the door to the ambulance for Andrew and got in after him.

Andrew watched as Zeke opened a drawer and pulled out a large bag. He ripped it open and took out a plastic shell, then nodded toward Drew's wrist. "Lift that away from your body."

The pain when the air cast was placed around his wrist brought Andrew out of what was left of his alcohol-induced haze immediately. Zeke carefully inflated the air cushions of the brace and pulled the valve after ensuring the brace gave enough support to his damaged wrist.

"Damn it, Hollister, date much?"

Andrew opened his eyes and leveled his stare at the doctor. "No. Why? Don't all first dates end with an unconscious ex and an ambulance ride to the hospital?"

Zeke chuckled and checked the vitals of the man lying on the gurney. Drew pulled a deep breath. For some reason, he couldn't find an ounce of empathy for the stupid fucker. Zeke annotated the clipboard next to him before he responded, "Actually, dinner and a movie are the standard first-date go-to's. Although, I do think you've got a pretty damn good chance at a second date."

A smile spread across Andrew's face as he closed his eyes. "True."

Ken walked up behind her, closing his notebook after talking with a few of the town folk. "Well, time for me to hit the road. I have a buttload of paperwork to do thanks to that idiot. Gen, I'm charging him with felonious assault with a deadly weapon. I'll need to get a statement from you, but it can wait until tomorrow unless you'd rather do it now."

"I can give you the statement now. It is short and sweet. Drew and I were at the bar, we decided to come back to my place. We stopped here and Avery called out to us from the street. Drew pushed me behind him. I stepped to the side because I don't follow orders very well and saw Avery swing the bat at Drew. He lifted his left arm to deflect the blow and swung once, hitting Avery with his right fist. Avery went down like a load of bricks. Drew's wrist was broken by the bat, and boom, you were here."

"All right. I'll work with that and stop by tomorrow to get that in writing. If you can, jot it all down tonight while your memory is fresh." Ken shook his head and rubbed the back of his neck. "Can you imagine how mentally unbalanced that moron had to be? Who in their right mind would use a baseball bat against a mountain of a man like Andrew Hollister? He was just asking to get his ass kicked." The deputy walked to his car and turned off the emergency lights after he got into the vehicle.

Allison stepped up onto the sidewalk. Gen's friend was in her pajamas. She put her arm around

Genevieve's waist and gave her a hug. "You realize first thing in the morning, I am coming over, and we are having coffee. You are definitely filling in all the blanks."

Gen couldn't help the cynical laugh that bubbled up. Her life had been turned on its axis today, and Drew had righted it all this evening. "Coffee in the morning sounds great; see you when you get here."

She walked to the back of the diner, ran up the stairs to her apartment, and retrieved her cell phone. Avery hadn't arrived in Hollister, South Dakota, by accident. There was somebody working an agenda behind the scenes, and she knew who that was.

Gen dialed her father's number and waited for an answer. Her mom answered the phone. *Great.* Not the person she wanted to talk to right now. She swallowed her anger and spoke, "Mom, I need to talk with Dad."

"What?" Miranda was obviously pulled from a deep sleep, her refined Southern accent rough and scratchy. "Genevieve, are you all right?"

She spoke slowly, trying to hide the bitter edge in her voice. "Yes, Mother, no thanks to Avery. He came after me tonight with a baseball bat to try to force me to come back to Alabama. If my friend hadn't been with me, God only knows what he would have done."

"What? He did what? He attacked you with a bat? Are you okay? Oh, my God, honey!" Her mother's voice shook, and she could hear her father's demanding questions in the background.

"He is being arrested and charged with assault with a deadly weapon. The deputy sheriff who lives in this town saw the whole thing. Avery tried to take out my friend, but he is a former Marine. He dropped Avery with one punch."

"Honey, you are on speakerphone. How in the hell did that weasel of a man find you?" Her father's demand was the crux of the entire situation.

Gen waited for a count of ten to give her mother a chance to speak up, but when she didn't, Gen spilled the beans. "Mom gave him my address. He showed up today and made a horrible scene in front of the entire town. Plus, he said some disgusting things about me, and he was shown the way out of town by my friend. Tonight, when my friend Andrew and I were walking home, Avery attacked us. Andrew stood in front of me and took the blow with the bat. Andrew countered with a right hook to Avery's face, and he was knocked out immediately. The deputy sheriff had just pulled up and witnessed the entire thing."

"Princess, you have my word I will do everything I can to make sure your young man's medical and legal bills are paid and he doesn't lose any wages because of his injuries." Her father's voice was controlled and measured, and she could tell he was very angry. He had also taken her off speakerphone.

Gen huffed a tired sigh, "Daddy, that's sweet, but I don't think Drew needs your money. I will let him know you offered it, though."

Her father's voice softened. "All right, princess, just let me know what I can do. I will get ahold of Avery's family and let them know my displeasure and keen interest in that twit's every move. Gus Montague may have powerful connections, but I don't need support from people like him if he can't control his son. I have some PR work to do. Do you know how far your mother is involved in this little scheme?"

"No, I only know she mentioned Avery the last time we talked about two weeks ago. She wanted me to bury the hatchet for the good of your campaign."

"Dear Lord. When will she ever learn?" He sighed deeply. "If your mother's involvement in his actions is implicated or even implied it could get ugly for my future endeavors."

Her shoulders dropped as she pulled her hand through her hair. She was suddenly very tired. "Thank you, Daddy, I love you. I will call you if I have any updates."

"Okay. Good night."

"Daddy?"

"Yeah, honey?"

She looked down at the floor and sighed, "Mom really thinks that I can't do any better than Avery."

He made a tsking sound. "Sounds to me like you are doing just fine without any help or interference from your mother. Good night, princess."

CHAPTER 9

Gen sprinted to her cell phone when it rang at five in the morning. She was down in the diner's kitchen getting things organized so she could be gone for the day. The sign she'd taped on the front door probably wasn't needed. Knowing the grapevine in Hollister, those who didn't know what happened last night soon would. At least Edna would know not to come looking for gossip at the diner.

"Hello?"

"Ms. Wheeler, this is Andrew Hollister. I understand you have my son's truck?"

Gen gulped and nodded even though the man couldn't see her. "Yes, sir. He asked me to drive it to Rapid and pick him up today."

"Doctor Johnson called and told me they were going to repair the broken bones in surgery and cast him. Andrew called our ranch foreman and asked for a fresh set of clothes to be brought in to you. Apparently, there is blood on his."

"Probably from when he hit Avery. Did Zeke tell you what happened?"

"No." The comment was concise and abrupt.

She wasn't surprised. Zeke was probably busy with two patients. "Oh, well, Drew and I were walking back from The Bit and Spur to my apartment over the diner when someone from my very distant past went crazy and took a baseball bat after Andrew."

"Is that crazy man still alive?" Senior chuckled.

Gen smiled for the first time since answering the phone. "Yes, sir, but damaged. One punch from your son was all it took."

"Figures. Andrew is one tough cookie."

"That he is."

"So, he was out with you. In public?"

Gen blinked. "Should I be offended by that question?"

"No, not what I meant. My son hasn't been very social since he returned from the Marines."

"We went to have a drink before we came back for dinner. We've been seeing each other in the morning before the diner opens for about two weeks. We're friends."

"Friends. That's… that's good. Ryan is bringing in clothes for Andrew. When you get to the hospital, if you could ask him to call me, I'd appreciate it."

"I can do that, sir. Thank you for having Ryan come all this way."

His father cleared his throat. "I look forward to his call."

"I won't be in Rapid until later this morning. I'll have him call."

"Appreciate it." The line went dead.

She looked at the phone for a moment before she slid it into her back pocket. There was a tension between the two men, but it seemed like Drew's father was trying. Hopefully, Drew would meet him halfway.

Four-and-a-half hours later, Gen pulled Drew's huge king cab 4x4 truck into the parking lot at Rapid City's Regional Hospital. She stopped at the information desk and asked for Andrew Hollister.

"Are you family?" the snippy woman behind the counter asked.

"No. I brought him the clothes that he asked for and I'm here to pick him up."

"You can wait over there." The woman pointed to the waiting area.

Gen glanced at the empty area and then back to the woman. "Why?"

"It's not visiting hours." The woman lifted an eyebrow and pointed to the sign behind her. "It's Saturday. No visitors until one o'clock."

"One?" Gen repeated just to make sure she heard correctly.

"That's correct."

"Yeah, no. That's not going to work for me." She pulled her phone from her back pocket and dialed Zeke's cell.

"Hello."

"Hey, Zeke, it's Gen. I'm at the front desk. They won't let me up until one. Visiting hours."

"Give your phone to whoever is at the desk." Zeke sounded tired and grumpy.

The woman took Gen's phone and sighed, "Hello." She straightened and sent a glare in Gen's direction. "Yes, sir." She handed the phone back to Gen and snipped, "He's two floors up from here. Room three-forty-one. That elevator."

Gen channeled every ounce of Southern charm she had and replied, "Bless your heart, you've been most kind." Which meant, 'Screw you, lady,' in southern.

The elevator opened into the ward directly across from the nurse's station. Zeke was talking with a very pretty nurse, their heads close together as they examined a chart. He saw her and smiled. "I am glad you showed up. Andrew Hollister has to be the world's worst patient." He looked directly at Gen. "Would you please get in there and try to talk reason to the idiot?"

Gen looked toward the door Zeke motioned to. "Be glad to. What am I supposed to get him to do?"

"The man is checking himself out of the hospital AMA. He really needs to have someone keeping an eye on him for the next couple days. I recommend he not be released until tomorrow."

Gen smiled at the obviously tired doctor. "I will do what I can, Zeke."

She walked across the hall and into the private room. Andrew appeared to be asleep. She put his clean clothes on the stainless steel rolling table that was positioned by the door. Her attention riveted on Andrew's massive body. His frame dwarfed the metal bed. The printed hospital johnny was obviously too small and laid open at the back but covered his muscled chest. She examined the sleeping man, taking in his masculine beauty. He was magnificent. His dark hair and thick eyelashes accentuated his high cheekbones and strong features. The shadow of his beard gave him a rakish quality. She shivered at the memory of his kiss sending delicious tingles of electricity through her. He was obviously dreaming, his eyes jerking restlessly behind his eyelids. His arm muscles jumped, and his breathing was fast and shallow.

Gen reached up and moved his hair off his face. At her touch, he jumped and grabbed her hand in a crushing grip. His eyes opened, searching wildly. She winced at the pain of his grasp but leaned into him. "Drew, it is okay, no one is going to hurt you." She watched him swivel his head, taking in the hospital room. He relaxed his hold on her hand but didn't let it go. His intense eyes bored into hers until he drew a deep breath and lay back on the mattress, closing his eyes. She reached up with her other hand and caressed his cheek.

He opened his eyes again, his breathing ragged. "Get me out of here, Gen. I can't stay in a hospital again. Get me out now."

"Why, Drew? Why do you need to leave?" She sat on the side of the bed and lowered her hand to his chest, feeling his heart race.

He closed his eyes and shook his head. Licking his dry lips, his statement said it all. "Please."

"Okay. I'll be right back." She leaned up and kissed him softly, pushing his dark hair away from his eyes.

Drew sat up when she stood. The hospital gown they had draped over him dropped to his lap. The blanket covered his lower half, but she could see the damage that had been inflicted on his body.

She stopped dead in her tracks at the foot of his bed, looking at the rippling muscles of the man sitting up. He was chiseled perfection. She smiled at him, her eyes devouring his body, the Marine Corps tattoo on his left bicep dancing when he moved his arm. "Lord above, may I cash my rain check in now?"

He chuckled and rubbed his face with his good hand. "That depends on if you're able to spring me from this place."

Gen let her eyes wander over his chest again. "I'll be right back."

She headed out of the room and found Zeke. "I'll watch him, but we need to get him out of the hospital."

"That's not in his best interest."

Gen glanced around. "Zeke, I walked in when he was having a nightmare. This place is bringing back bad memories. He's just started coming out of whatever self-imposed isolation he was in. He can stay with me. I'll watch him. You're in town and right across the street. If I need help and you're not there, I'll call Eden."

Zeke rubbed the back of his neck. The dark circles under his eyes told of a sleepless night. "Okay, but only on the condition he stays with you for the next forty-eight hours. No ranch work, no driving, and sure as hell no more fighting."

"I'm sure that can be arranged." Gen smiled at Zeke and spun on her heel, heading back into Drew's room. "Okay, I arranged a jailbreak, but on the condition you stay with me for the next two days. Zeke wants you in close proximity to medical care should you need it."

Drew's eyebrows rose as he looked at Gen. "Are you okay with me staying at your place?"

She walked up to him and put her hand on his thigh and said softly, "I was the one who suggested it."

He reached for her and pulled her close, kissing her softly.

Zeke cleared his throat from the door. "I am going to do the discharge paperwork. Is there room enough in that truck for one more? My SUV is still parked at The Bit and Spur."

Gen turned and looked at him. "Yes, there's plenty of room."

He nodded. "Get some clothes on him. I will send in a nurse in a moment with a couple of pain pills." He lifted a finger and pointed at Andrew. "You will take them; the ride home will jar the hell out of that wrist." He muttered to himself as he walked out the door.

Drew dropped his legs over the side of the bed, his thighs and calves just as defined as his upper body. Cords of heavy muscle popped when Gen put her hands on his knees and stood between his legs. Her nails trailed up his thighs and under the blanket. She could feel the scars on his legs, but her eyes held his. The heat of his erection radiated to her hands. She looked down at the impressively tented blanket and then back at him, smiling seductively.

He cupped her face with his right hand. "If your fingers go any further north, we are going to have an explosion."

She smiled and took a deep breath. "Okay, cowboy, I'll back off… for now." She leaned forward and kissed him softly, running the tip of her tongue over his bottom lip.

He pulled away. His breath was ragged as he whispered, "If that is backing off, we definitely are going to have problems."

"Excuse me, Mr. Hollister. The doctor wanted you to take these before you checked out." The nurse's face was morbidly red as she held out the little white paper cup toward Drew.

Gen pulled away from him, took the offered cup,

and smiled at her. "Thank you, I will ensure he takes them."

The nurse ran her eyes appreciatively over Drew's body before she said, "The discharge paperwork is done, and Zeke has gone to change. I suggest you do the same." She smiled at Drew and left the room.

Frowning, Gen followed her to the door and shut it firmly behind her. Turning, she picked up his clothes from the table and brought them to the bed. She pulled a pair of black boxers out and held them up. "I have a feeling I am going to enjoy the next couple minutes." She watched as he pulled the blanket back, exposing his erect, thick, long cock. The deep red crisscrossed scars were unimportant to her. She grinned wickedly at him. "Cowboy, I really, really need to go for a ride. You are magnificent."

"And you are good for a man's ego."

"You shouldn't need any bolstering."

He sighed, and a sad look traveled across his face. "Believe me, my ego has been nearly nonexistent. Until you." He smiled, stood, and stepped into the boxers as she held them for him. She felt her hair brush against his thighs as she lifted his boxers. He put his good hand on her shoulder to steady himself. He pulled her close as soon as she lifted the waistband to his hips. "God, what you do to me. For me."

A knock at the door made her giggle. Drew yelled, "Just a minute!"

She reached for his jeans and held them so he could

step into them. They fit low on his hips and molded to his fantastic thighs and ass. She put her hands on her hips, stepped back, and looked at him. "Damn it, man, I just want to take them off again."

He chuckled as he reached out and lifted the hem of her sleeveless shirt. He ran a finger under the soft fabric at the waistline of her jeans. "The feeling is mutual."

Grabbing for his black T-shirt, she turned around and helped him ease his casted wrist into the sleeve and pulled it down over his luscious abs.

She'd have been lying if she didn't admit she wanted him, but the most important thing was to get him out of the hospital. She went to the closet and pulled out the clothes he'd worn last night. It took a few seconds to stuff them into a plastic bag that she found hanging from a hook in the closet. Taking his boots, she walked over and put a finger on his hard chest, moving him back onto the bed. She stood between his legs and had him lift each foot as she put a sock and boot on each. Bending over, she pulled the jeans over his boots. Finished, she turned around and smiled at him. He grabbed her and wrapped her in his embrace, the cast hard against her back.

His low voice rumbled, "Woman, when you bend over... God, your ass is perfect, absolutely perfect. That's probably crass to say, but damn." His hand went under her shirt and settled on her hip. "God, Gen, you're amazing."

The knock at the door sounded again but this time with attitude. Drew dropped his hand and shouted, "Come in."

Zeke walked through the door. Dark circles under the doctor's eyes punctuated the exhaustion that etched into the lines of his face. Zeke glanced at the pills still in the paper cup and picked them up. "Damn it, Andrew, take the fucking pills."

Andrew looked at him and smirked. "Rather testy today, aren't we, Doc?"

Zeke handed him a glass of water. "Yeah, going without sleep for forty-eight hours will do that to you. Can we go? I am going to crash in the truck."

Andrew took the medication and stood up, putting his arm around Genevieve's waist. "Take me home."

"I will, but you need to call your dad on the way. Before those pain pills take effect." Andrew rolled his eyes, and she shook her head. "I promised him. Don't make a liar out of me."

Andrew frowned. "He called you?"

"He did. He's worried about you." They walked out of the room together because Andrew flat out refused to ride in a wheelchair, and down the hall where Gen pushed the button for the elevator. Zeke almost sleep-walked behind them to the truck.

Andrew didn't say anything until they reached the truck. When everyone was strapped in, she put the truck into gear and headed to the interstate. "Call your father."

KRIS MICHAELS

Andrew sighed heavily but placed the call.

"Sir, you wanted me to call?" Andrew stared out the side window so she couldn't see his expression. "Yes, sir." He listened for a moment more. "No, I'm discharged, but I'll be staying in town for a couple days." He nodded and then added. "Yes, sir, with Gen." Andrew glanced at her and then out the side window. "A lawyer?" Andrew chuffed out a laugh. "Of course, he has. Ken Zorn saw it. I'm not the one who started it. It was self-defense." Andrew listened for a bit more. "Yes, sir. Goodbye."

"A lawyer?" Gen glanced at him as she merged onto the interstate.

"Seems one Avery Montague is alleging I instigated the event."

"Dear Lord above. I can call my dad. He can put a stop to it."

Andrew chuckled and dropped his cell phone into the cup holder. "Don't worry about it. Dad's already called his lawyer. Your ex doesn't have a leg to stand on."

A gentle snore from the back seat made them both glance back. Zeke's head rested against the door and his mouth was open a bit. He was out like a light.

"My offer stands."

Drew yawned and leaned back in his seat. "I know and I thank you."

She smiled as the miles turned under the wheels of

the truck. She wished last night hadn't happened, but because of Avery, they'd gotten closer faster than she would have imagined, and for that, she was grateful. Was that selfish? Oh, hell yeah, but she wasn't going to apologize.

CHAPTER 10

Genevieve pulled behind the diner into her driveway and stopped the truck. She looked in the rear seat and smiled. Zeke was sound asleep. She looked down at her lap at the man sleeping peacefully. The medication had knocked him out about twenty minutes into the drive. He'd made no pretense and lay across the seat, putting his head on her lap as she drove.

Carefully she put her hand on his shoulder and shook him gently. "Hey, cowboy, we need to go inside now."

He opened his eyes and gazed at her, obviously still under the effects of the medication. His pupils were dilated, and he couldn't keep his eyes open.

Zeke jumped and sat up, rolling his neck. "Damn, that was the fastest trip to Hollister I've ever had."

"You were out before we hit the interstate."

"Exhaustion will do that to you. Let's get this guy inside." Zeke jumped out of the back seat of the truck. He opened the front passenger side door and helped Gen get a disoriented and slightly loopy Drew up the stairs to her apartment.

Gen led the men to her bedroom, and Zeke controlled Andrew's flop on top of the white, silk-covered, down duvet. She pulled off Andrew's boots and covered him with a chenille throw. Following Zeke out of the bedroom, she shut the door quietly.

Zeke reached into his pocket and gave her two brown vials of pills. Lifting one, he said, "These are for inflammation. If we keep the swelling under control, it will allow the healing to start sooner. This bottle is for pain. I doubt he'll take them. If he doesn't, give them back to me, and I'll dispose of them properly."

"Thanks, Zeke, you're a good man." Gen smiled up at him.

He massaged the back of his neck and started down the stairs and out of her apartment. "Yeah, find a good woman and tell her that for me, would you?"

Gen laughed at him, "There is someone out there for you, Zeke."

He turned and looked back up the stairs at her. "I'm not so sure." He opened the door and walked out.

And that comment hurt her heart. Zeke was a damn good man. Attractive and nice.

She walked back into the bedroom and stared at the man sleeping on the bed. It was only four in the afternoon, but she was dog-tired. Gen shrugged out of her clothes, slipped into her satin pajamas, and crawled under the throw with Andrew. Forward? Yes. Did she care? No. She cuddled next to him because forward or not, she needed sleep, too. She sighed deeply and closed her eyes, happily falling asleep to his deep, steady breathing.

Drew woke slowly from the drugs, and the softness of the body beside him initially confused him. He lifted his head and looked down at the woman next to him. He blinked several times, looking around the room, orienting himself. *Must be her bedroom.* He stretched and slipped out of the bed, quietly walking to the adjoining bathroom. He used the bathroom and lost his jeans and T-shirt, leaving on his boxers before he padded back to the king-size bed and slipped back under the throw that covered both of them. Reveling in the feel of her soft warm skin next to his, he ran his thumb over her nipple, caressing her gently through the satin of her pajamas. Her body reacted immediately; the nipple puckered and hardened. He switched his attention to the other and watched her body respond again. Her hips pushed back toward him, and she opened her mouth and sighed heavily in her sleep.

Drew moved and rolled her gently onto her back. In her sleep, she immediately turned toward him and his warmth. He smiled and lowered himself to her breast. His tongue circled and pulled it into his mouth sucking tenderly, wetting the satin. Her body arched toward him, and her hands reached for his hair, threading her fingers through it. Clothes disappeared as their desire flamed.

Her moan acted like pure gasoline on a fire that threatened to consume him. He lifted up on his good arm and looked down at her. Her eyes were halfway open. The smoking, sultry desire that emanated from her hit him like a bullet piercing its target. He ran his finger over her lips. "You are beautiful."

She took his index finger into her mouth, sucking it, laving it with her tongue. He kept his finger in her mouth as she lifted off the mattress, straddling his body with hers. She released his finger and bent down, pressing her breasts onto his chest. "I am cashing in my rain check, cowboy. I don't want to wait any longer. Unless you're not feeling it." She rolled her hips against his erection.

"I'm feeling it." God, was he feeling it. The sensations were almost painful. He prayed he didn't... *No!* Those thoughts were not welcome. Not now.

Gen narrowed her eyes, obviously seeing something in his expression. She leaned forward and whispered, "I want you. Now, hard, deep, and fast." Lowering her lips to his, she invited his tongue into her mouth.

He cupped the back of her head with his hand and pushed into her warm mouth. He used his tongue to take her the way he wanted his cock to take her body, rough and filled with passion.

She moaned against his assault, and her tongue danced with his. His cock ached as she pushed down on him. Pulling away from his kiss, she reached for his cock, positioning so his shaft would enter her sex.

He grabbed her hip before she could slide down on him. "Gen, it has been a long time. I'm not going to last."

She bent down to him and kissed his collarbone as she whispered, "Cowboy, just let me touch you. God, you are so thick and big."

He tightened his grip on her hip. "I don't have a condom."

She smiled. "I am on the pill, and I want you. Now… let… me… down."

He released his grip on her waist, and she circled his cock with her hand as she centered over him. Gen lowered slowly onto his shaft. He reached to where they were joined and found her swollen clit. Drew applied pressure to her sensitive nub with his thumb. She slid down his cock slowly, her body stretching to take his girth. She moaned and shuddered before she rocked her hips back and forth on him. His orgasm built faster than her body could accept him. Her voice floated down to him as she panted, "God, Drew… oh, God…"

He felt her velvet core grab him as her body squeezed his cock. He held her hip with his good hand. It took only minutes before they both came. Her body sucked at his cock, a rhythmic spasm that grasped both her body and his. Gen's moans turned to gasping cries, feeding his orgasm. Drew's own guttural shout joined her as he came deep within her. The overwhelming physical release caused by heat pulsing from every fiber of his body was intensely painful yet so immensely pleasurable. He pulled her down on top of him, his breath coming in ragged pulls.

Gen's body shivered as she lay on him, his hard muscles heaving under her body as he too struggled to breathe again. She kissed his neck and stroked his cheek. "I think we have a problem."

He froze, his hand caught in her hair. She lifted herself up on her forearms as she gazed down at him. His eyes searched hers before he spoke. "What problem do we have?"

She traced his lips with her finger. "I've never had an orgasm. You, sir, have set a standard. Can you continue to do that, or am I to be disappointed?"

Pulling her down to him, he breathed his response in her ear, "You have set a higher standard, Gen. I haven't been able to make love to a woman since I was injured almost two years ago. You have saved me from the corner of hell I've been living in. You've healed me in ways I never thought I'd be able to mend. I thought..." He lifted so she could see his eyes. "Thank you for being who you are. For not giving up. I don't have the words."

Tears filled her eyes; she drew a shaky breath and turned to offer him her lips. The kiss was soft and gentle, his sense of urgency replaced with a slow, sensual burn. He flipped her onto her back and settled between her legs. He kissed her breasts, pulling her nipple into his mouth. He lightly bit on her swollen bud, causing her back to arch off the mattress. His desire grew with each moan or whimper she made. Her hands roamed his back, shoulders, and arms. As he kissed his way to her wet folds, she entwined her fingers in his hair. He kissed and licked the inside of her thighs, teasing her by blowing on her hot sex as he switched to the other thigh.

Her legs stiffened as he entered her with two fingers. Her hips lifted toward his mouth as she moaned, "Drew… please!"

He chuckled as his lips kissed her thigh. "Not yet, babe." He spread her and found her hard clit, drawing the sensitive nub into his mouth. Her hips catapulted toward him as he continued to manipulate her sex with his teeth and tongue. Her hips bucked against his mouth, the rhythmic clenching deep within her nearing a crescendo.

Drew lifted his head and kissed her leg. "Come for me, baby, I want to taste you." He lowered his head and used his tongue to plunge inside her in an unrelenting assault. He felt her body tremble and then contract as she came.

"Drew! Oh, God!" Her head thrashed from side to side as her body tightened in release.

When she stilled, he kissed his way back up her body, stopping to pay particular attention to her breasts. He lifted off her, and with his good arm pulled her to the edge of the bed. Her black hair flowed behind her as he looked down at her soft, beautiful body. Standing beside the king-size bed, he lifted her legs over his shoulders, centering himself on her wet heat.

Gen opened her eyes, the desire smoldering as she looked at him. "I need you inside me."

He carefully entered her; the tightness of her sex captured him in intensely hot folds. He pulled out and entered her again, going deeper. Her hands fisted the duvet under her as his pace remained deliberately slow. He fought to control the release his body craved.

Their crest hit almost simultaneously. Her orgasm was what he was waiting for as he released himself and took her wildly and freely. His sharp, rapid strokes sent her over the edge again, and this time, he went with her.

Drew sank down onto the bed and pulled her close to him. Spent, he buried his face in her hair. "You are amazing, Gen."

She sighed and hummed something in reply before

she snuggled next to him, softly caressing his chest with her fingertips. She stilled almost immediately.

He kissed her hair. Exhausted, he closed his eyes, too. Gen had unlocked his prison doors. He had no doubt getting out of the confines of his personal hell would take longer, but for now, this unlocked door was enough. Gen was enough.

CHAPTER 11

Gen awoke against the hard muscles of the man next to her. Her stomach rumbled loudly as she realized she hadn't eaten since breakfast... yesterday. She looked at the clock and smiled. It was almost nine at night. Slipping out of bed, she slid into her long terry cloth robe and padded out to the kitchen. She pulled the casserole she'd brought up before she'd gone to Rapid out of the refrigerator and put it in the oven. Yawning, she also put water on to boil. Getting out a tea bag and cup, Gen waited for the water to boil and pulled her phone from her purse. Her mother and father had both called. She sighed and hit the button dialing her father. Her mother could wait until tomorrow.

He answered the phone on the first ring. "Hi, princess."

She smiled. "Hi, Dad. What's up? Why did you call? Mom called, too." She picked up the tea kettle as it began to whistle and poured the water over her tea bag.

"Your mother called to apologize. Believe me, I will keep a close eye on her, and she will not be making any more ill-advised decisions based on her perception of my best interests. Her association with Avery and his subsequent felonious actions at her behest could cause me serious problems."

Gen's back stiffened. "Mom told him to attack us?"

Her father sighed heavily. "No, that's all on Avery; at least, that's what your mother is professing."

"You know he's alleging that Drew attacked him. Dad, he won't win that. I was there. The deputy sheriff was there. He attacked us."

"He's doing what?" Her father's surprise was apparent by the sharpness of his question. She related what she'd heard of Drew's conversation with his father. "I'll handle this. What the hell is Montague doing? His idiot son could ruin his political aspirations, and I won't have any mud splashed on me even if it means distancing myself from your mother. Again."

Gen lifted the tea bag. And watched the water darken. "Did she say why?"

"A political powerhouse reunited." The sarcasm dripped from her father's comment.

"She needs help, Dad."

"I know. I... yes, I know. I'll take care of her. How is

your friend?" Her father changed the subject and she allowed him that out.

Gen heard the floor creak behind her and turned around to see Drew standing in his jeans, sans anything else, leaning against the door jamb. His white cast was lifted and resting on his other arm. She walked toward him and stopped directly in front of him. Leaning forward, she filled her lungs with his scent. She placed her head on his shoulder as she spoke, "My friend's name is Drew, and he is an amazing man. He had surgery on his wrist. He is doing remarkably well."

"Good, princess, I want to thank him personally when he is able to get up and around." Gen looked up at Drew, who could hear her father clearly. He smiled and raised his eyebrows at her suggestively.

She cocked her head at Drew and spoke, "Oh, he is up and around, so I will let him know. I love you, Dad."

"I love you too, princess." Her father ended the call.

As she hung up, Drew pulled her to him and kissed her softly. "I woke up and realized I was alone. Not exactly what I was hoping for."

She smiled and traced the muscles of his shoulders with her fingertips. "I thought for sure my growling stomach would wake you up. I don't know if you ate today, but I haven't."

He shook his head. "Just crackers and water after surgery last night so I could get the damn IV taken out."

She nodded toward the oven. "Jambalaya."

"Good. I'm starving." He sat on the kitchen counter and pulled her in between his legs, trapping her by linking his ankles at the back of her knees.

He pulled her hair gently and she looked up at him. "Is this mess with your ex going to cause your family problems?"

She shook her head. "The only one in any hot water is my mom. If she is implicated in sending him up here and his bone-headed actions there could be ripples, but Dad said he was ahead of the situation and taking care of her. I am sure he is assigning a handler to Mom to keep her under control. I love him, but she needs help, and he's ignored it for most of my life."

A knock at the back door was the only warning they got before Jeremiah opened the door and stepped into the kitchen. His eyes popped wide. "Wow, okay. Am I interrupting something?"

Andrew glanced at him. "Not at the moment."

Gen chuckled at the comment and patted his leg, stepping away from Andrew. "What are you doing in town this late?"

"Ah, I have a patient being driven in early tomorrow morning. I need to do an evaluation before he goes to his rehab stint. I was hoping I could crash here until I had to go across the street."

"Sure, you know where the guest bedroom is. We were just going to eat. Would you like some jambalaya?"

"When have I ever refused your food?" Jeremiah rubbed his hands together. "What can I do to help?"

Both men pushed away from the table, rubbing their stomachs. Jeremiah moaned, "God, Gen, I love your food."

She took the last of the dishes and rinsed them in the sink. "Compliments will get you invited again. The bed is made up, you know where everything is." Gen put the last plate in the dishwasher and moved behind Drew. She put her hands on his shoulders. "You, sir, have to take an anti-inflammatory for your wrist, those fingers are swollen. The pills are in my bathroom."

They both looked at her but didn't move. She put her hands on her hips. "Gentlemen, if I have to repeat myself there will be hell to pay." Both men stood and went different directions. Gen smiled to herself and turned off the light behind her. "Smart boys."

She followed Drew into the bedroom and waited for him to come out of the bathroom. He stopped in the doorway, looking at her.

Holding his eyes, she walked across the room and stopped inches from him. He moved to put his arms around her, but she stopped him.

"Oh no… my turn, cowboy." She lifted the T-shirt over his abs and pulled it off. He once again tried to capture her. Laughing, she took his hand and tugged it as she led him to the bed. She pointed to the mattress. "Hands above your head, cowboy." His eyes flashed as he laid down and slowly raised his arms above his head.

She reached for the button on his jeans. As she unfastened the anchor, she went to her knees and kissed the scars previously hidden by the material. His body tensed, and she heard him suck in a sharp breath of air. Unzipping his jeans, his swollen cock released itself from the fabric. She pulled the material down over his hips and thighs, leaving the jeans at his feet. "Going commando are we, cowboy?"

His chuckle died as she raked her fingernails down the underside of his cock. A shudder ran through his body. Gen lowered her head and followed her nails with her tongue. His cock stiffened under her trail. Following the sensitive skin under his shaft, she retraced her initial caress and finished by licking his cockhead. She could taste the pre-come that moistened the tip. Her eyes darted up to look at him. "Do you like this?"

"Oh yeah, I like it." His eyes were dark, and she could see the need in them.

"Tell me how you want it." She licked her lips and lowered her head to his cock again, circling the tip with her tongue. She kissed the sides of his cock and held his balls.

His body jerked several times as she circled his

crown again. "God, Gen, take me in your mouth." She lowered herself over him and hummed against his cock as she sucked just the cap into her mouth, laving the crown with her tongue.

His whisper was intense, "Oh fuck! More, suck me, please." She adjusted her position and opened her throat, lowering herself on his massive cock. She used one hand to fondle his balls as the other stroked up and down in rhythm with her mouth.

"Jack me harder with your hand, Gen." Her hand clenched him tighter, stroking him. He lowered his hand to her hair and fisted a large handful. "Can you take me deeper?" His hand pushed her down further over his cock.

Gen relaxed the muscles in her throat and allowed him to push her head down, his cock buried deep in her throat. As she lifted, she took a large breath, allowing him to control the pace. He was lost in sensation, and she let him drive his cock into her throat. When his legs trembled under her hands, she held her head back and filled her lungs with air. She took him down her throat as deep as she could and stopped. She deliberately swallowed, constricting the muscles of her throat around him. His reaction was instantaneous. "Nggghhhaa!" His orgasm spewed his seed deeply down her throat. Her eyes watered and her lungs burned, but she waited until he had finished before she pulled off him and gasped for air.

He sat up and lifted her onto the bed with him. Holding her tightly, he kissed her. His hand shook as he pushed her hair away from her face. "God, Genevieve, I have never felt anything like that before."

She smiled and kissed him softly. "I wasn't sure if I could do it. I read it in a romance novel I bought last month."

He looked at her, his face blank, not comprehending. "A romance novel?"

She giggled, "Yeah."

He pulled her into him. "Woman, I will build you a library and buy you every romance novel in print if you promise to do that again."

She put her hand on his chest and snuggled closer. "Deal, cowboy."

Drew saw Frisco walk through the opening. The trip wire glistened in the desert sun, but Frisco wasn't paying attention. Drew ran as fast as he could. He screamed Frisco's name, waving his arms to get the man's attention. His scream was lost in the explosion of the bomb's percussion. The initial blast once again threw him past a small half-wall. The pain of his lower body being pierced by hot metal tore through him. The whine in his ears deafened everything else, even the gunfire surrounding him. The stench hit him first. Blood, sulfur, and dirt. Voices screamed for help. He sat up, seeing the remnants of his men in the debris of the explo-

sion. He couldn't move. He couldn't get to them. Why couldn't he move?

Drew snapped into a sitting position and pulled ragged gulps of air into his lungs. Her movement next to him spun him in her direction. Gen's long, dark hair spread over the pillow, her face soft, lips parted as she slept. Drew closed his eyes. The fucking dream again. *Again.* He pulled on his jeans and walked out to the front room. He froze at the realization someone else was already in the room.

"Chill, it's just me. I couldn't sleep." Jeremiah was lounging in the recliner.

Drew let out a long breath. "Know that feeling."

"Yeah? What feeling is that?" Jeremiah's voice was calm and inviting.

Drew chuckled, "Oh, hell, no, Doc, I am not going there with you."

"Oh, so there is a *there.*" Jeremiah leaned forward in his chair.

Drew threw him a pissed-off glare. "Get out of my head, man, you weren't invited."

"Yeah, cause if I were invited, I would tell you 'there' is an actual place in your mind. We would build a map of 'there,' examine why you are stuck 'there,' and find an exit for you. But that is only if I was invited."

"You're not." Drew dropped onto the couch and stretched out. He turned toward the man in the recliner. "What nightmares are keeping you awake?"

"Nightmares, huh? From your time in the Corps?"

Drew ran his hand through his damp hair. "What the fuck, man? I was just having a conversation. This is exactly why I don't like talking to people."

"Amazing, isn't it? I am extremely good at what I do." Jeremiah's soothing voice irritated Drew.

"Yeah, then why the hell aren't you doing it somewhere other than Hollister?" His growl caused a chuckle from the chair in the corner of the room.

"Honestly?"

Drew lifted his head and looked at the man, "I don't do anything but honest."

"All right. I moved here years ago after a situation. I was inside a supermax facility when riots erupted. I witnessed a serial killer at work. Actually, I was forced to watch, and I couldn't do shit about it. It fucked me up. I left and started over."

"Holy shit, sorry. Gen told me about the shit at the prison. Tactless of me to throw it in your face."

"I appreciate the apology, but it isn't necessary. The facts of my past are what they are. I dealt with it."

Drew scrubbed his face and sat up. "PTSD is a bitch... or so they tell me."

Jeremiah chuckled, "Based on the scars on your abs, I would say you know firsthand."

Drew looked down at his low-slung jeans and shrugged. "It was worse."

"But you are still stuck in your place." The quiet statement lingered.

"Yeah, just about every fucking night." Drew's body relaxed. He stretched out on the couch again, and Jeremiah sat back in his chair.

"Andrew, I can give you some help escaping the hell you keep putting yourself in."

"Putting myself in? Are you fucking insane? I don't willingly go there! Fuck me, man, I would give my left nut never to relive that day again." Drew hissed the words across the room.

"Yet your mind takes you back 'there,' your emotions lock you in 'there.' We can unlock that cage and you can walk away from that place."

"I talked to the Marine shrinks. It didn't help."

"When? Right after the event? No, it probably didn't. They probably prescribed some neuroleptic drug that made you agitated and gave you waking terrors. Right?"

Drew lifted his arm off his face and looked at Jeremiah. That *had* happened. It was fucking horrible. How did this guy know? He shrugged and hedged, "Maybe."

Once again, a laugh of derision came from the darkened corner. "I can help you. I am not going to prescribe meds or make you lie on a couch."

Drew lifted his head off Gen's couch, waved to his prone body, and flipped him off, causing Jeremiah to laugh.

"The offer is there if you want it."

"Yeah. Thanks. I'll think about it." He rolled off the

couch and went back into the bedroom. He'd consider it. Man, anything to get away from thoughts of that day.

CHAPTER 12

Gen finished telling Jeremiah about Avery's morning visit to the diner and put a bite of pancake into her mouth.

Jeremiah's jaw tightened before he ground out, "That prick Avery. If I ever see him again, I am going to knock him out." Jeremiah's words were laced with venom.

Drew's eyebrows rose and Gen slapped her hand over her mouth, trying to stop laughing.

"What? What is so funny?"

Gen covered her mouth and chewed quickly before she answered, "Drew beat you to the punch! Literally." She swallowed hard and grabbed her milk.

Jeremiah turned to Drew. "Excuse me?"

Drew shrugged. "He treated her like shit. I threw him out of the diner."

Gen interrupted and explained, "No, he really

means that! He picked him up and tossed him out of the diner into the street. The entire town saw it." She mimicked the action.

Jeremiah blinked and turned his head to stare at Drew.

Drew shrugged and continued as if the event wasn't newsworthy. "Anyway, he showed up as we were coming back here later that night. Had the balls to take a swing at me with a baseball bat. I blocked the bat with my left arm." He lifted the short cast and sneered, "This happened. So, I hit him with a right."

Gen nodded. "With one punch, Drew broke Avery's nose, his jaw, and he messed up his head when he bounced off the sidewalk. Ken Zorn saw the entire thing and arrested Avery for felonious assault with a deadly weapon." She shook her head. "Both Avery and Mom need help."

"Yeah, I will call Dad and try to get him to get her into therapy. Again. Avery is on his own. The asshole. So much for our sleepy little valley. I saw the cast last night. I just figured you did something to your wrist at the ranch. That's what I get for assuming." Jeremiah chuckled, "The things that happen in this town."

Drew leaned forward. "Sleepy valley or not, what this town lacks in population, we more than make up for in personality."

"Indeed. It is why I stuck around. Thanks for breakfast. I'm going to head across the street and talk with Zeke. He's been just as strapped as I have been since the situation at the Marshall Ranch. Eden wants to know if he needs a day off."

"Which means I get the kids. Yay!" Gen clapped her hands.

"Which means you get the kids after you close up. Speaking of which, Jay wants to know if you've finished watching that movie. He wants to watch it again."

"I have. Let me get it." Gen popped into the living room and grabbed the DVD. "Tell him to bring it if Eden needs to fill in and we'll watch it again."

"He'll have the lines memorized." Jeremiah lifted the DVD and saluted them both with it. "Thanks again for the hospitality."

"Anytime," Gen said as her brother shut the door behind him.

Drew walked up behind her. "I need to work off some of that breakfast. Any ideas?"

She turned and put her arms around his neck. "I have one or two ideas, Mr. Hollister."

He dropped his lips to hers. "Really, could you be more specific, Ms. Wheeler?"

She looked at the granite island in the kitchen and then back at him.

He smiled slowly. "I think I like the way your mind works." He held her close and walked her backward as he kissed her. His tongue danced with hers until he pushed her toward the island. Lifting his lips from hers, he stepped away.

"Take your clothes off for me. I want to see you." Drew stepped back and leaned against the counter as he waited.

Gen's hands trembled. Uncertain and suddenly embarrassed, she felt her face heat. His eyes were heavy-lidded, and he was looking at her expectantly.

"Take off your shirt, Gen." His words were low and commanding. Mesmerizing. Pushing away at the embarrassment, she slowly lifted her t-shirt over her head. She held it in her hands, not sure what to do with it.

"Drop the shirt." His voice wrapped around her. She did exactly what he asked. "Take off your jeans." Slowly, she unbuttoned the jeans and shimmied out of them, leaving them pooled at her feet. She stared at him and waited. This game was something she could enjoy.

He lifted his hand and made a motion for her to spin around. Closing her eyes momentarily, she swallowed and took a deep breath. She stepped out of her jeans and slowly turned around for him. Once again, she faced him and waited. "Bra and panties." The deep rasp of his voice caressed her like his lips and tongue had last night. Slowly, Gen removed her bra, allowing her hair to fall over her breasts. The panties were the work of a second as they slid to the floor.

Drew stood away from the counter and walked toward her slowly. Using the fingertips of his good hand, he lightly touched her waist, causing her skin to flinch and her body to tighten in anticipation. He walked all the way around her slowly. Her heart raced, and her body ached for his touch. She could feel heat forming in between her legs. He was making her want him with just this… examination.

"Beautiful." Moving her hair off her shoulders, he exposed her breasts and lightly touched her nipples. The buds puckered and tightened. Her breath caught in her throat at the sensation of his rough skin.

"Face the island and put your hands across the top. Hold the other side." She looked up at him; his eyes appeared almost black as he stared at her. The intensity and sensuality that radiated off him became a tangible sensation. Slowly, she turned and walked to the island. Gripping across the top of the island, her breasts pressed against the cold granite as her ass lifted, exposing her sex to him.

"Close your eyes," his voice commanded. Gen gasped at the feel of his hand on the small of her back and closed her eyes obediently.

She heard his clothes fall away from him and waited. A soft touch on the outside of her hip and then his mouth on the back of her thigh. Gen's gasp of surprise filled the room.

"Shh… so beautiful. Don't move." He kissed the back of her other thigh and spread her legs further. His hand pulled her legs even farther apart. She felt his lips work toward her center and then avoid it, moving back toward her ass where his hand rested. His kisses traveled to her tight hole. The feel of his tongue rimming around her caused her to tighten and gasp his name.

"Shhh, baby." He kissed and licked her tight pucker. "I am going to take you here one day. Not today. Today I am going to kiss and touch you everywhere. Learn your body, what makes you hot, what makes you crazy. I'm going to see how far I can take you before you lose control." His lips traveled her body, possessing and exploring. He flipped her only after he'd done exactly what he said he would.

Lifting her onto the island, he made her put her arms above her head and stared at her. "Just like that, baby. Lay just like that." Starting at her ankles, he licked, kissed, and nipped his way to her center but gave her sex no attention. Then his assault started at her shoulders, lowered to her collarbone, then he feasted on and fondled her breasts, nipping at the swollen buds. His lips traveled lower, and her body shuddered hard.

Gen's breath came in shallow pants. She'd never been the object of such intense attention. She wanted him to take her, to finish what he was teasing, but he lifted before he reached her sex and moved back, lowering his lips to hers. She begged for what he was denying her. Not with words but with small cries, sighs, and whimpers.

Lifting away, he gazed at her before he lowered once again to her breast and almost violently pulled her nipple into his mouth, sucking furiously. Gen's entire body tightened and convulsed; her orgasm ripped from her along with her gasping cry. His hand cupped over her core tightly, and she shoved and ground against him as her orgasm collapsed around her.

Drew pulled her to the edge of the island. "Wrap your legs around me, baby." Her body reacted automatically, doing what he asked. Lifting her with his good arm, he walked them to the wall and leaned her back against it. Lifting her over his cock, he centered under her. Allowing her to slide down his cock, he sucked in a hiss of air as she sheathed him.

His cock drove into her, forcing her into the wall as his hips pumped rapidly. He growled as he released. Wedging them against the wall, he held her up. She ran her fingers over his shoulders. "I'll never be able to look at that kitchen island again and not think about what just happened." She dropped a kiss to his shoulder.

"Damn, woman. You're addictive."

She chuckled. She wasn't anything special. "No, I'm just me."

"And you are more than I deserve, but damn it, I'm going to hold on."

She dropped another kiss onto his shoulder. "Me, too. As tight as I can."

CHAPTER 13

A ndrew walked out from behind Gen's diner. She'd closed the diner on Monday, and they had spent the entire morning and most of the afternoon getting better acquainted. A smile flashed across his face. It had been a wonderful escape, but he had to face the town sooner or later. Leaving Gen in the kitchen to prep for the morning's crowd, the first person he ran into was Phil Granger. The man crossed his arms and cocked his head. "You did good the other day, Andrew. That rat needed to be skinned. Anyone that could talk like that about one of our own deserved everything he got and then some."

Andrew stopped beside the man he'd known most of his life. Phil's wife Sarah and he had graduated a year apart. Phil was about ten years older than he was. "I appreciate you helping Ken with crowd control."

Phil chuckled. "Seems to be my lot in life. Directing traffic."

Andrew lifted an eyebrow. "Don't you mean directing people?" Phil Granger had a way of picking people to do things with or without their knowledge. When Phil got an idea you were right for a job, there was no stopping him from promoting that agenda. A talent scout for the town of Hollister. That should be on Phil's sign instead of 'Mechanic on Duty.'

"I may resemble that remark," Phil laughed. "It's good to have you home again. Don't be a stranger."

"I'm trying," he admitted.

"Keep after it. She's worth it." Phil nodded toward the diner as he spoke.

"She is," Drew agreed and walked across the street.

Father Murphy walked out of Sanderson's Market as Andrew was entering. "Andrew. Good to see you. How's the wrist?"

"Doing well, sir." He lifted the white cast. The swelling had gone down thanks to the medication. He kept it elevated at his waist because he wasn't going to wear a damn sling as Gen had suggested.

"Good, good to hear it. I must say there has been a lot of excitement in town lately."

"Sorry about that." He cringed a bit.

"Don't be. You did what you had to do. That fellow was spoiling for a fight. We don't need that type around here. Tell your father I said hello and that he should come see me."

"With a bottle of fine Irish Whiskey?"

"All the better. It has been a long time since we indulged in that earthly pleasure. Good day to you, son."

"Good day." Andrew ducked into the small market and nodded to Allison Sanderson, who was behind the counter. The woman's red eyebrows lifted. He let it go and headed to the small section that had pain relievers. The smell of fresh-baked bread immediately reminded him of his grandmother's cooking. It always did. He took a deep breath, grabbed an extra-strength variety pain reliever, and headed back to the counter.

"Hurting?" Allison nodded to his cast.

"A bit." He wasn't going to take any of the painkillers Zeke had given Gen.

"Surprised Zeke didn't give you something for the pain." She rang him up, and he paid in cash.

"He did. I don't like narcotics." He never had.

Allison nodded. "It's good to see you, Andrew. Been gone too long."

"Thank you." He took his small box of pain relievers and exited the market.

Instead of going back to the diner where Gen was working, he turned and headed to the medical building. He walked in and listened to a lot of nothing. Finally, he heard footsteps. Jeremiah smiled at him. "Andrew. Zeke's not here."

"I know. I watched him leave before I went to the

store for this." He tossed the bottle of over-the-counter pain reliever in the air.

"Then, you stopped by to…" Jeremiah let the question trail off.

"I don't want to be stuck there anymore. I want to be better. For myself and your sister." He didn't drop his eyes. He wouldn't be ashamed of asking for help.

"Excellent." Jeremiah sat down on the corner of the reception desk. "I can talk for a bit now, and we can schedule appointments for us to discuss what's going on."

"I'd like that."

"Okay. Come on back." Jeremiah led him down the hall, and he was pleasantly surprised to see two large wingback chairs. There was a large leather couch along the back wall. Andrew looked at it and then back at Jeremiah, arching an eyebrow in question.

"Oh, come on, having a couch is part of my professional heritage. Besides, it is comfortable enough to sleep on. Have a seat." Jeremiah pointed at one of the wingback chairs.

Andrew sat down. "No drugs."

Jeremiah stalled halfway into his seat and looked at him. "Noted." He lowered into the chair. "What questions do you have for me?"

"Questions?" Andrew blinked. "I thought you were the one to ask questions."

"True. But usually, my new clients like to know what type of therapy we're going to use."

"Do you know what type of therapy without talking to me?"

Jeremiah smiled. "You're very astute. No, I don't, so let's start with some basic questions. Where does your dream start? The one you've had for what was it, almost two years?"

Andrew nodded. The guy was sharp and had a hell of a memory. "Yeah. Almost two years." It would be two years in thirteen days. But who was counting?

"Does your dream start the same way every night?"

Drew cast him a quick glance. "Yes, it never varies."

Jeremiah nodded. "Tell me, what is the first thing you remember seeing in your dream?"

Drew sat silently. The minutes ticked by as he relived that fucking dream. Each time it started, he saw the same thing. "The trip wire."

Jeremiah leaned forward. "All right. I am sure you read the reports on the incident you were involved in. Was the actual explosion, not the one in your dream, caused by a trip wire?"

Again, the silence stretched as he recalled the reports he'd read. They were all wrong. Wrong according to what he'd lived night after night. "No. The report said it was an IED triggered by a pressure sensor that exploded two mortars buried next to it."

Jeremiah cocked his head before he asked, "No trip wire?"

Drew shook his head but didn't answer.

"So, what happens next in your dream?"

"The wire is broken, the explosion, and all the fucked-up mess afterwards."

"Who trips the wire? You?" Jeremiah sat quietly.

Andrew closed his eyes and forced himself to answer, "No, Frisco trips it. I try to warn him, but he doesn't hear me." The anguish he felt bubbled to the surface where it sat raw and exposed.

"Good. But in the report, according to accounts of the other people who were there, where was Frisco during the actual explosion?"

"Beside me, to my right."

"Was Frisco injured or killed that day?"

"Yeah."

"Which was it? Injured or killed?"

Drew stood up. "Fuck this, I need to go."

"You can go, Andrew. You can run away. It's worked well for you so far, hasn't it?"

Andrew clenched his right hand into a fist repeatedly. Fuck, Jeremiah was right. It wasn't going to change a damn thing if he didn't try to figure out why he was having these nightmares. "Frisco was killed."

"How? According to the reports, please."

Drew turned and stared at Jeremiah. "His body was riddled with shrapnel and thrown on top of me, over my head and chest when the bomb exploded."

"In your dream, does someone throw themselves on top of you?"

Drew's head shook. "A wall stops the blast in my dream."

Jeremiah nodded. "All right. I know you don't want to talk any more about this today, but I *can* help you. How about you let me try?"

Drew lifted his chin. "Nobody but us will know?"

"I don't discuss my clientele with anyone. You can enter from the back, which keeps prying eyes out of your business, too."

Andrew nodded and then tossed his new doctor a question. "How are you going to treat my issues, Doc?"

"People's memories are always skewed, either by emotion, perspective, or morality. Additionally, memories aren't recollections of the actual event, rather recollections of recollections, so each time we access these memories, they are changed. Imperceivable to your mind. I can't be certain, but the going-in bet is your dream may be your subconscious trying to reconcile itself against your memories of the event. Hypnosis would allow you to walk through the actual events of the day while shielding you from the emotional cost associated with it."

Drew snorted, "Hypnosis? Is that a legitimate therapeutic avenue?"

"Yes, it is. Eventually. We have a lot of work to do before we get to that point, though." Jeremiah nodded. "So, I'll see you next Tuesday? Does morning or afternoon work better for you?"

"Last appointment of the day, if I can. The ranch is busy in the morning."

"You've got it. I'll see you here at four next Tuesday."

Drew extended his hand. "I appreciate the help."

"We all need help every now and then," Jeremiah assured him. "It won't be easy, but we'll get you out of 'there.'"

Drew nodded and walked out of the medical building. He strolled back to Gen's diner, greeting a few people on the way, but he didn't stop to visit. The conversation he'd had with Jeremiah made him think. Gen's brother had a way of getting him to say things. His defenses had been up for so long. Trusting anyone to get close? That would be hard. Everyone except Gen. She melted his defenses with a smile, disarmed him with her laughter, and he gladly surrendered to her. That woman was his piece of heaven; he'd claimed her.

CHAPTER 14

Allison trotted across the street as soon as Gen turned on the lights in the front of the diner.

"Hiya, you're going to need help this morning. Mom cut me loose so I could bus and pour coffee."

"Your mom is a smart woman. At least my psycho ex is going to make me some money." Gen snorted and handed Allison an apron. "I'll pay you."

"Bullshit. I'm here for the show." Allison poured herself a cup of coffee and made her way into the kitchen.

"I made two extra sheet pans each of caramel and cinnamon rolls. Same with the biscuits. After this weekend's events, there is no doubt every busybody, gossip, and curious bystander in the Tri-County region will come by for the scoop."

"You're going to be slammed. The business is doing really well."

She nodded, "Sometimes too well. I am seriously considering hiring someone to help me full-time. I'm at work at four-thirty every morning, and by the time the prep work is done for the next day, it is late. I know the wintertime is slower, February and March I handle alone just fine, but I almost double my breakfast sales in April. Lunch is steady at fifty to sixty meals if you count takeout. But this," she motioned to the kitchen and diner, "is starting to get bigger than just me."

Allison nodded, set her coffee cup down, picked up the heavy sheet pans of rolls, and handed them to her. "Do you need someone with experience, or are you going to train them?"

Gen shrugged as she took one sheet pan at a time from Allison and put them in the oven, setting the timer, "I didn't have experience when I opened. If I hire someone, I can teach them what they need to know. Do you know of anyone who needs a job?" Gen looked at her and grabbed her coffee.

"One or two people come to mind, but no one that I'd recommend as trustworthy." Allison made a face and grabbed her coffee. "What do you need me to do?"

"Right now, drink your coffee. Once the people start coming in, we'll be going nonstop. When the front coffee urn runs dry, use the back one to fill the carafes and restart the front. I have a feeling we're going to go through twice the usual amount."

She wasn't wrong. The diner swarmed with people, so much so some were forced to take their orders to go.

The president, vice president, and secretary of the combined Catholic and Presbyterian's Ladies Circle decided to grace the diner this morning. Gen chuckled at the way Allison sweet-talked each of the elderly ladies.

When Drew walked into the diner through the kitchen, it was as if the world had suddenly stopped spinning and people were frozen in time. Complete silence ensued. Gen looked up from pouring coffee to see what had caused the constant din of conversation to cease.

Andrew walked to her where she stood behind the counter. Pulling her into an embrace, he lowered his mouth to hers and kissed her soundly on the lips. He pulled back and smiled. "Heading to the ranch, see you tonight."

She smiled and winked at him. "Dinner is at seven, cowboy."

He lowered his lips to her ear. "I am looking forward to dessert."

She gasped and then he smacked her on the ass. "Oh no, you didn't!" she yelled after him.

"I think I did," he yelled back as he exited through the kitchen.

Gen turned around and stared at the people in the diner who stared back at her.

She lifted her arms and asked, "What?" A smattering of laughter rolled around the small diner, and Allison's voice started conversation going again. Thank goodness for her friend. Gen felt her face flush, but it was a wonderful feeling.

The morning crowd lingered a little longer than usual, and she had just finished clearing the last three occupied booths when Ken Zorn walked in.

"Morning, Ken! Hopefully, the last couple nights have been quiet for you." She poured him a cup of coffee as he sat down.

"Thankfully. I was able to get most of my paper-work done. Your ex has an initial court appearance this afternoon that I am going to attend. Seems he has himself some fancy corporate lawyer up from Alabama. The shyster hasn't passed the state bar here, though, and he hired my brother-in-law as his legal representative."

Gen's mouth dropped open. "Your brother-in-law?"

Ken nodded as he drank his coffee. "Damn straight, I put them in jail, and my sister's husband gets them out. Not much fun at our family reunions."

"I could see where that would cause a conflict."

"Good times. Do you have any caramel rolls left?"

"I do. I made extra today." Gen spun and headed into the kitchen. She was back in an instant, setting the dish down in front of the deputy. "They just came out of the oven, so be careful."

Ken nodded. "Our little hamlet has been busy lately. But I still say this is the best place on the face of the Earth to start a family and raise a passel of kids. If you can find the right woman." He chuckled and looked up at Gen. "Or man, in your case."

Gen pushed his shoulder. "Don't marry me off just yet, Ken; I don't have a good track record. Your court case today is evidence of that."

Ken laughed. "This town has enough gossip from this weekend to keep those old birds squawking for at least a year." His radio sounded with something unintelligible. He unclipped his microphone and spoke into it, then turned to her. "I have to go. Can I get a box?"

"Sure, here you go." She put his roll into a white takeout container and poured him a large to-go cup of coffee, dropping several containers of cream and sugar into a small bag.

Ken took out his wallet, but Gen stopped him. "Consider it a thank you for being in the right place at the right time Friday night."

The surprise on Ken's face was genuine. "You know, I still can't figure it out. The stupid clod is in jail with his jaw wired shut, a broken nose, two black eyes, and one hell of a headache. What part of Andrew did he think he could get the better of? That man lacks all sense of judgment."

Allison called out from the kitchen, "No shit." She appeared in the passthrough. "He cheated on Gen, and then attacked the largest walking wall of muscle I have ever seen. I would love to analyze his brain under a microscope when he dies."

Gen snorted a laugh. "So, we are a neurobiologist now, are we?"

Allison smiled broadly. "You bet, sweetheart, I'm that neuro-whatever-thingy, a waitress, clerk, cowgirl, dishwasher, best friend, and old maid, all rolled into one." She laughed and looked around the nearly vacant diner. "You got to admit that has to be some sort of record for most professions held by one woman at the same time. Where are the judges for Guinness Book of Records when you need them? I'm simply amazing if you ask me!"

Ken laughed as Allison disappeared back into the kitchen. "Really, Gen, she is hurting in the self-esteem department. You need to work on that. I'll stop by after court and let you know what is going on, not that I anticipate any issues." He walked out of the diner and tipped his cap to Edna Michaelson as she entered the establishment. Gen glanced knowingly at Allison, who had made her way back out to the front of the diner.

"Hi, Edna. What brings you over so early?"

"I have a loose schedule this week. May I have a cup of coffee?" The woman took stock of the nearly empty diner.

Gen poured her a cup and motioned to the empty tables. "Take your pick."

Edna sat down on the first stool at the counter. "Thank you. According to all accounts, your ex is a dick."

Gen's mouth dropped open. "Excuse me?"

Edna waved her hand in a dismissive fashion. "Why not call a spade a spade? He was horrid to speak that type of language. I witnessed the entire thing. Whatever did you see in him to begin with? And I'm sorry if I offended you." Her tone clearly stated otherwise.

Gen wiped up the coffee she had inadvertently spilled on the counter as she laughed, "Don't apologize, he is a dick, and I'm pleading brain damage. I don't know what I saw in him."

Edna took a sip of her coffee. "Good. Andrew is a much better match for you. As a matter of fact, your ex and Andrew's ex should meet. That would be a winning combination for sure."

Gen turned to look at Allison. "Andrew has an ex?"

"Crap. Edna, why are you stirring the pot?"

Edna harrumphed an inelegant sound out and then quipped, "She is an ex, right? Gen doesn't have anything to worry about."

Allison nodded. "Yeah, nothing at all. That bitch Stephanie Howard. Some fiancée she was. She was sleeping around on him while he was gone. Heard the sugar daddy she had dumped her for a younger model recently. Mom says she is coming back to town. Maybe we can hook up those two and drive them out of town."

Gen couldn't help asking, "Allison, how long were Andrew and his fiancée engaged?"

"I don't know, they grew up together, were high school sweethearts, and it was just kinda assumed they would get married. Don't really know when or if it ever became official."

"Good riddance to both of them, I say. Has anyone heard what the hell was happening last week? I can't find out a thing."

"I really have no idea, Edna." Gen shrugged innocently.

Allison leaned forward. "Edna, I wasn't going to say anything, but I heard that the men who were here were from the government and they were investigating an alien aircraft sighting."

Edna blinked and then narrowed her eyes at Allison. "You're making fun of me."

Allison took a finger and crossed her chest. "Honest to goodness, Miss Edna. They had a UFO sighting. That's why they were here one day and gone the next. Real hush-hush Area-Fifty-One-type stuff."

"Really?" Edna put down her coffee cup. "That makes sense." She stood up and grabbed her purse. "I have an errand to run. Good day." The bells on the door rattled as Edna swept out of the diner.

Gen laughed out loud, "Allison, that was outrageous."

Allison snorted. "Serves the old biddy right for bringing up Stephanie. That was over so long ago. There is nothing there, Gen. That, I can promise you."

"Girl, exes are a byproduct of life. I'm not worried." She grabbed Edna's cup and took it to the back and stacked it in the wash rack.

"I wish I had an ex. Hell, I wish I could find anyone in this town… or the state, for that matter." Allison leaned against the wall and watched as Gen started the dishwasher and ran the rack through.

"Girl, you are very attractive, there has to be a guy out there that is secretly in love with you." Gen walked up and gave her friend a hug.

Allison laughed and shook free from Gen's embrace. Her dark auburn locks flowed around her shoulders. "Looks are only skin deep, as my daddy says. Someone would need to love me for the real me, you know, the," she made air quotes as she continued, "opinionated, brash, non-mouth filtering, deer-and-pheasant-hunting, cussing 'cause I like to, country hick. I don't think there is a man in the county that has the balls to take me on."

"Don't give up. I promise there is someone out there for you. Now, are you working the lunch shift? If so, you can make the salad."

"You couldn't pull me away. I want to see how many people are talking about aliens."

The lunch crowd was every bit as large and curious as the breakfast crowd had been. Gen and Allison busted tail, serving and keeping up with the orders. When the door was shut after the last customer, Gen locked the door and walked into the kitchen.

Allison pushed a rack of dishes into the dishwasher and shut the door, pushing the button to start the cycle. "You need to hire help. Even with me working back here, you were racing around like a madwoman. Is it always like this?"

"No, this was an extremely busy day. But I agree, I need to hire some full-time help. I'm running the business in the black. I don't owe anything on the building, I bought it outright with part of my inheritance. The land I'm leasing from the Hollisters and the profit is good."

"Never be embarrassed about being successful. Just do what the Hollisters and Marshalls do. Help behind the scenes when you can; nobody is the wiser, and you'll feel better about being rich."

The afternoon passed quickly as Allison helped Gen prep for the next day's breakfast and lunch menu but focused primarily on the morning work. Gen locked up the lower portion of the building and Allison met her in the backyard with a beer. "I put the rest of the six-pack in your refrigerator upstairs. Here's to eight alien sightings."

Gen laughed. "Thanks, I can use one, and you were wicked."

They sat down at a small picnic table and visited as they watched birds playing in a huge cottonwood tree that shaded the back of the building. Ken Zorn pulled up her driveway in his squad car and walked over to them. "Got one of those for a cop who is off the clock?"

Allison nodded. "I need a refill anyway, what about you, Gen?"

She shook her head. "No, I'm good." Allison headed upstairs and Ken looked directly at Gen.

"Your ex is out on bail for now. His lawyer tried to convince the judge Andrew beat him after he attacked Avery. That was until I took the stand. When he started poking at me, trying to allude that I would misrepresent the truth, I gave the defense the camera feed from the dashboard that I use for DUI recordings. I hit it as soon as I saw the bat come out of the car. It showed everything. The windup and homerun swing and Andrew's one and only defensive counterpunch were perfectly framed. It ran until the ambulance arrived and I walked over and turned off the recording. Needless to say, your ex will have to do some very inventive dancing to stay out of jail."

Gen shook her head. "I still don't understand why he would do such a thing."

Allison walked outside with two more beers and sat down. "Heard anything about the alien sightings?" She took a swig of the beer and then smiled at Ken.

"Do I even want to know what that means?" He looked from one to the other. Gen laughed and filled him in. "Dear Lord, only you, Allison," Ken chuckled. "Don't ever change, life would be dull without you."

"That's me, local comedian. Hey, did you hear Stephanie Howard is coming back to town?" Allison asked the deputy.

"Heard it. She's got some nerve, but then, we were all young once." Ken shrugged. "Mistakes of our youth and all that crap." Ken stared straight at Allison. "For-giveness should be a thing."

Allison lifted an eyebrow. "Not sure about that." She chugged the bottle and set it on the table. "I'm out of here. See you later, Gen. Thanks for the fun today."

"Thank you for helping me," she shouted after Allison's retreating form. She turned slowly and looked at Ken.

"What?" The man took a drink of his beer.

"What was all that about?"

"All what?" Ken set his bottle down.

Jeremiah walked into the backyard. "Can I get one of those?"

"Fridge. Upstairs." Gen watched him trot up the stairs.

"Seriously, there was some kind of hidden message going on between the two of you. Do you two have a history?"

Ken chugged the rest of his beer. "I'll be heading home now. Just wanted you to know what was going on. And Gen, you don't need to worry about Stephanie. Water under the bridge."

"What's water under the bridge? I'm not chasing you away, am I?" Jeremiah sat down on the picnic table.

"Nope, I'm heading home and getting some sleep before I get called out tonight. Full moon. Things get crazy." Ken walked back to his car and pulled out of the drive.

"What was water under the bridge?"

Gen filled him in on what Allison had told her about Stephanie.

Remi lifted an eyebrow. "From a strictly unscientific point of view, you and Andrew have almost identical experiences with your fiancés. From a psychiatric standpoint, that has so many ramifications, I could feather my retirement nest if I were to delve into them."

Gen snorted. "I'll save you the trouble, Remi. We are both probably a little gun shy about commitments but know we both want someone who will stick with us for the long run. We want a life with someone who will not cheat. How did I do?"

Remi took another drink. "Damn it, I think you just stole my future Porsche."

CHAPTER 15

Gen jumped when her cell sounded. She'd just finished showering. She and Andrew had fallen into a wonderful routine. He'd work at the ranch and come back into town for dinner and spend the night with her.

"Hello?"

Andrew sighed, "Hey, we have some issues out here. I'm not going to make it for dinner. Could be a long night."

"I'll put the spare key under the big rock by the stairs. I don't think I would sleep if the door wasn't locked or you aren't here." Avery hadn't contacted her again and he should be back in Alabama, but she wasn't going to take any chances, not until the matter of his assault was dealt with and history.

Andrew's deep voice caressed her ear, "If I can get into town tonight, I will."

"Be safe. If it gets too late, sleep at the ranch. We can be apart for one night." She whispered the words, not liking them but knowing it was the right thing to say.

"We can, I just don't want to be."

"Me either, I was just being responsible." She laughed, and so did he. "Good night."

"Good night. I'll come in as soon as I can."

Gen smiled and hung up. She glanced around her apartment. She hadn't realized how empty it felt without Drew. She shook her head. "That didn't take long, did it? You're hooked on that man." She nodded to herself. She was, and she wasn't going to apologize to anyone about that fact. Sighing, she put her hands on her hips and stared at the small room off the kitchen. "Well, laundry, it looks like it is you and me tonight." She turned on the television to something mindless. The night was quiet, and she managed to finish her laundry, clean the apartment, and scrub down the shower before she locked up and went to bed.

When the alarm went off, she was still alone. She sighed and got up. Getting ready to start another morning's work without the possibility of morning sex with Andrew sucked, but it was a routine she knew. Hair up in a ponytail, dressed in her diner uniform, she trotted down the stairs and started work.

The breakfast crowd came and went. Edna Michaelson held court in the large corner booth. Several of her cronies had books on Area Fifty-One. She couldn't help smiling as she served them.

"Hey, Gen."

Gen glanced up from pouring Edna's second refill. "Dixon, how have you been?"

"I'm doing well. I was wondering if you had any of that vegetable fried rice left. My wife is having cravings."

"Well, congratulations. Come with me, I think we can find some." Dixon frowned but followed her into the kitchen. She grabbed his arm. "You've got to warn everyone at the ranch. Edna Michaelson was fed a line of poo and is running with it. She swears the reason for all the activity a couple weeks ago is because a UFO was sighted."

Dixon blinked and then a smile spread across his face. "All right. That's... fantastically weird, but hey, whatever it takes."

Gen swatted him. "Don't egg her on. Those old ladies are already ordering books on UFOs." She opened her walk-in freezer and went to the back. "I have vegetable fried rice and some tofu dumplings."

"God, yes. Anything you can give me that is meat-free. She's getting over morning sickness and is ravenous."

"When are y'all expecting?"

"Just over seven months." Dixon smiled again.

"Well, congratulations, and if she has cravings for anything, let me know and I'll make up a batch so you can take it home. It's easy for me to make an order."

"Thank you so much. What do I owe you for this?"

"Nothing except your promise you won't egg on Edna and her crew."

"I'd rather pay you. Messing with them could be fun." Dixon gave her an evil laugh.

"Out." She pointed to the front of the diner.

Dixon laughed and headed out of the diner.

"Mr. Marshall, could we have a moment of your time?"

Dixon smiled at the women. "Sorry, ladies, my pregnant wife is craving what I have here so I'm making tracks."

Dixon winked at her and made his way out of the diner.

Working through the morning and lunch crowd, Gen had just waved goodbye to the last patron when Drew pulled up in front of the diner. He got out of the truck and marched inside. His face was hard as stone as his eyes swept the diner. "Can you close?"

"I was just about to. What's up?"

"Please. Now. I need to talk to you, upstairs." The electric tingle of fear ghosted over her. "Is everything okay?"

He shook his head, not saying another word. His jaw was clenched, and his good hand folded into a tight fist.

She locked the door, put the 'Closed' sign up, and headed into the kitchen. She put lids on pans and made sure the ovens and stoves were off. "I'm ready."

He grabbed her hand and almost pulled her out of the kitchen and up the stairs. He didn't say anything when they reached the apartment. Instead, he pulled her into her bedroom, shutting the door. Andrew pulled her T-shirt over her head and unbuttoned and unzipped her jeans. His mouth clasped over hers tightly as he pushed her back onto the bed. Using his good hand, he expertly released her bra and then pulled her panties down. His lips never left hers as he reached down and unbuckled his belt, freed himself from his jeans, and drove his cock into her. His arms held her tightly, and she melted into his need, pulling him closer to her.

His mouth took hers, his tongue claiming possession of hers and demanding her response, and she responded. Gen's body ached for his touch, but this wasn't their normal coupling. This was different. He needed something from her, and whatever it was, she would try her damnedest to give it to him. Her hands circled his back and pulled him closer to her. His good hand lowered and coaxed her body as he repeatedly drove deeply into her. Her body tightened and convulsed around him, her sounds suppressed by his dominating possession of her mouth. He finally lifted his mouth and growled out her name as he emptied himself into her. Drew pulled her to him and held her so tightly she had difficulty breathing.

She didn't understand why he was so desperate for her, but she did know he needed her in his arms. Wrapping her arms gently around him, she stroked his back and kissed his chest gently.

"Drew, what is wrong?"

He shook his head and pulled her against him tighter. Gen felt his shoulders shaking and realized he was crying. Her instinct took over as she pulled him toward her. "I'm here. I'm right here." She rubbed his back and kissed him.

His voice was almost a whisper, "He's dead, Gen."

She froze. "Who? Who did you lose?" She whispered her question.

"Jose. My gunnery sergeant. He committed suicide yesterday afternoon. His wife called me about an hour ago. She said he couldn't handle the pain. He couldn't stand it anymore. He ate a bullet, Gen." The utter desolation and grief in his voice hit her like a ton of bricks. Her own tears poured down her cheeks as she held him.

"I am so sorry, Drew. I'm here. You have me, you are not alone. I promise I'm here for you."

Gen held him long after his tears had stopped. She held him as his breathing leveled out. He was emotionally drained. Jose was a man Drew had spoken of often. Gunny was more than a friend, of this she was certain. A father figure perhaps, especially since Drew's relationship with Senior was so tenuous. She held him as he slept, his face finally relaxed and his body stilled. His pain had been so deep when he had come to her. She carefully covered them with her chenille throw and held him for hours before his body twitched against her and his muscles tightened. She shifted suddenly as he mumbled. He was dreaming again.

"Drew, you're all right. I'm here." She repeated her affirmations and held him tight as he dreamed. His breathing became labored, and he turned away from her, thrashing against the throw. Gen sat up in the bed and grabbed his shoulders. "Andrew, you need to wake up."

His good hand grabbed her upper arm as he suddenly sat up in the bed. The pain of his grip pushed a gasp from her, but she didn't move.

Andrew's eyes shifted around the room. His grasp loosened slightly as he looked at Gen blankly.

His eyes softened as he finally registered her presence. He laid back and pulled her with him. "I'm sorry babe. I'm so sorry." He kept repeating himself as he held her.

"You have nothing to be sorry about. You needed to feel alive, and you came to me. I understand. You lost someone very important to you and you're in pain. I'm here. There is nothing more important than making sure you're okay."

He pulled her face closer, and his deep, brown eyes studied her face. "I needed to have you. I needed to know there was something good in my life. He was my mentor. He pulled my ass out of so many fires and taught me how to be a good leader. He was always so strong, but bone cancer is a motherfucker." Drew's eyes closed. "The strongest man I know cashed it in."

She drew her fingertips across his brow and whispered, "The strongest man I know is grieving for someone he respected and loved. I can't make the pain go away, Drew, but I'm here for you, no matter what you need, no matter when you need it."

He pulled her close and kissed her softly. "He kept me alive, kept the squad alive. When the IED took us out, he put a bandage on his own leg, picked up that M4, and held cover fire until I could help him clear the field and patch up the men that lived. He fucking crawled to his position to overlap the field of fire."

"When did help come?" She drew circles on his back, not knowing what to do, just knowing he needed to talk and needed to know she was there.

"Later. Gunny passed out. Franklin was wounded badly; he was in and out of consciousness. The FNG was torn up and out of it but alive. When the Blackhawks finally descended, two of the responding fire team members on the ground were killed, but the other members of the team secured the landing zone and we were medevac'd out. I lost contact with Gunny and Pip at Landstuhl, they sent them stateside immediately. Pip died two days later. The FNG went to the mental ward, and I never saw him again."

"What does FNG stand for? Is it the guy's initials?" Her fingers continued to draw circles on his back as he held her.

He chuckled humorlessly. "FNG stands for 'Fucking New Guy.' The kid transferred in, and we hadn't even gotten to know him very well. His name was Barry, and he was torn to shreds by shrapnel. His body healed, but they told me he never came back from the explosion mentally. The kid is probably drooling into a bib somewhere; he couldn't deal with the reality of what he saw."

Her hands started massaging his neck and shoulders as she spoke, "So, you patched up the new guy and Pip before you helped the gunny protect your guys?"

His eyes closed as her hands continued to work on his tight muscles. "Yeah."

"And then Gunny passed out and you continued to fight even though you had the wounds that caused those scars?"

He nodded and replied, "Yeah."

"So, you continued to fight until help was able to reach you and extract your team."

His body froze and his muscles tightened again. "I…"

She kissed him softly. "You did everything you could. Gunny trained you well, you did what you needed to do, and you took care of your men."

He pulled away from her and put his arm over his eyes before he spoke, "Gen, if I had been a good enough leader, I would have avoided the IED. It is my fault they died."

She put her head on his shoulder and her hand on his chest. "Did you have any idea that the IED was planted there?"

He shook his head. "No, you don't get intel on things like that."

"So, you had no way of knowing the bad guys put the trap there, but when all hell busted loose, you did what Gunny taught you to do and you got the men who were left alive out." She lifted and kissed him softly. "You did the gunny proud, and you are still doing it. Gunny knew the good man you are, and he knew you'd take care of not only him but the rest of the men, too. When is Gunny's funeral? Can we drive, or do I need to make plane reservations?"

He lifted his arm and looked at her. "You don't need to go, Gen."

Her eyebrows rose. "I'm not going for Gunny. I'm going for you. You're going to go and be strong for his wife. You're going to say goodbye to a good friend, and when you are done, when your duties are finished and the dreams come, I won't let you be alone. I will be there for you."

A small smile spread across his face. "You have a business to run."

She scrunched her nose at him. "I do, but I also have a substantial inheritance and can afford to take a week or two off to take care of someone who means so much to me."

His hand lifted and stroked her cheek. "Who would that be?"

She smiled at her lover. "Do I need to say it? You, Andrew Hollister. You've worked your way into my life and into my heart. Be careful with it, cowboy. The poor thing was smashed into a million pieces once, it is very fragile."

His eyes gazed at hers. "Gen, I was engaged once, when I was young and stupid. I never loved her. She was someone I grew up with. I asked her while I was in college, before I joined the Corps. According to her, after I left, she was lonely, and she found someone else. Actually, if you believe some of the people in town, she found quite a few others. When I returned before I went into the Corps, she wanted to try to work things out. Since I never loved her in the first place, I just told her to leave, and she did. That was six years ago. I have never regretted asking her to leave, and I don't want her back in my life."

Gen rolled him over and pinned him down, straddling him. "You didn't owe me that explanation. We both have pasts. We made mistakes. The only thing I needed to know, you answered already. When I needed someone, you came to me. That tells me more than anything you could ever say."

His hand cupped her face and pulled her down to him. "You're here for me even when all I can do is take from you. I have never had someone hold me when I wake up from those damn dreams. I am fucked up."

She leaned down, closing the distance between them. "You aren't taking. I'm giving." And she'd give until he no longer needed the support. "Make love to me."

CHAPTER 16

Gen and Drew walked down the back stairs together. The kiss they shared at the bottom of the stairs captured all the need, the giving, and the desire the day had held. They walked through the diner, and she let him out the front door, locking it behind him. After he drove away, she made her way back into the kitchen and called her brother.

"What's up?" Jeremiah answered the phone and laughed.

"I need some advice." She stared at the stainless steel countertop as she spoke.

Her brother's tone changed immediately. "What is wrong? Is Avery back?"

"What? No, Avery is out on bail, and if he has any sense at all, he is still back in Alabama. No, Drew's gunnery sergeant from the Marine Corps committed suicide last night. We are going to Reno, Nevada, for his funeral."

"How is he taking it? Will he talk about it or is he closing himself off?" Her brother. She smiled. He was a wonderful man.

"We talked about it a lot. He is hurting, he loved that man, and it is hard to understand why he would take his own life. He dropped everything at the ranch and came in to be with me. That's a good sign, isn't it?"

Jeremiah was silent for a few moments. "Encouraging, yes. When do you leave?"

"We booked flights out from Rapid for the day after tomorrow. We'll have to leave at three in the morning to make it. Andrew went back to the ranch to pack and let his father know he'd be gone."

"I know I don't need to tell you this but keep an eye on him. This will be extremely stressful for him. If he needs to talk to me, have him call. It doesn't matter when."

"Why would he need to… oh." Gen closed her eyes. Andrew was seeing Jeremiah. Good. That was good.

"Shit." Jeremiah bit out the word.

"I'm not going to let on I know," she assured him. "But I'm glad he's getting help."

"No comment," Jeremiah grumped.

"Understood. Anyway, I wanted to let you know the diner is going to be closed and I'm going to be gone."

"How long?"

"As long as he needs." She didn't care. She owned

the diner, and if her clientele drifted away, she'd build it back up. Nothing was as important as Andrew.

Jeremiah's small hum preceded him saying, "Call me if you need anything."

"I will." They said their goodbyes, and Gen spent two hours throwing things away that would spoil while she was gone and giving the rest away to Phil and Allison. She posted a sign on the door, double-locked it, and turned off the lights. Tomorrow, she'd clean and make sure everything was taken care of, but tonight, she'd wait for Drew and take care of him the only way she knew how. She was going to love him.

The flights from Rapid City to Denver and then Denver to Reno were uneventful. When they landed, Andrew gathered their bags while she picked up the rental. She automatically upgraded the car from a compact to a full-size SUV. She chuckled at the thought of Andrew's massive frame fitting in behind the wheel of a small, hybrid car.

The trip from Reno to Fernley, Nevada, took less than an hour. Gen's hand was on Drew's knee the entire trip, making sure he knew she was there for him. He had pulled away mentally from her. She could tell the stress of the pending funeral weighed on him.

When they finally pulled up to their hotel, he checked in and unloaded the luggage, then pulled her into his arms. "Babe, I have to go get a regulation haircut. I can't wear my uniform with my hair this long."

Gen smiled and nodded, "I think I would like to see how you looked as a Marine. You go do what you need to do, and I'll unpack." She lifted to her toes and kissed him. "Come back soon."

He pulled her against him tightly and whispered against her lips before he kissed her possessively. "Thank you."

Since he'd learned about Jose's death, he'd been in a mixed haze of numb confusion. Well, numb unless he was with Gen. She made him feel. Away from her, an insulating fog surrounded him. So many emotions played through his mind that he didn't have time to examine one before another snapped up the previous' place. He fucking hated it because the one emotion that kept pushing forward was one that didn't make sense. He was so screwed. Had been since that day two years ago. He wondered if Jose knew it was the two-year anniversary of that fucking failed mission when he ate that bullet.

He gripped the steering wheel with his right hand and squeezed. He'd known. Would that day ever stop taking from him? Gen thought he was grieving. Maybe he was, only the feelings he was having, after the initial shock of Corrie's call, didn't register as grief. Fuck, he needed to talk to Jeremiah.

Drew pulled up to a barbershop with an old-time red-and-white barber's pole spinning in front of the door. He palmed his phone and looked at the screen. To what end? To have his emotions validated? How could anyone validate what he was feeling? Simple. They couldn't. He put the SUV in park, turned off the ignition, and pulled his ass out of the vehicle. He opened the door to the small, one-chair shop.

"Take a seat. I'll get to you as soon as these three are done." The old man snapped his directions. Andrew sat as commanded. When it was his turn, the old, grizzled barber snapped a white drape out and patted the chair before he barked, "What do you want, son?"

Drew cleared his throat, "Can you do a high and tight?"

The old man cackled, "Thirty years at Coronado, damn straight I can do a high and tight. You a Marine?"

Drew nodded, "Yes, sir, here to bury my friend."

The old man put his hand on Drew's shoulder. "Damn shame, son. How did you know him?" The white drape was snapped around his neck.

Drew pulled a deep breath. "I was his CO. He was a damn good man, pulled my young ass out of the fire more times than I could count."

The barber pulled out the clippers and put on the proper shield. "Tough, son. Sorry for your loss."

Drew watched as his black hair hit the cape and

then slid to the floor. The fact that he was here, getting a regulation cut, made things real. He didn't fucking want it to be real. He didn't know how to do this. To say goodbye. He'd been in the hospital when his men were shipped home and buried. He didn't get to say goodbye, to pay tribute to their service. Another failure that had been haunting him. As the barber shaved the back of his neck, he closed his eyes. He'd never imagined putting the uniform on again. He'd never dreamed of wearing the medals he'd earned, and he'd sure as hell never thought he would hang the one the President of the United States of America had awarded him around his neck again.

"How's that?"

Andrew looked up into the eyes of a man he'd once been. He nodded. "Thank you."

He pulled out his wallet and the man waved him off. "Thank you for your service."

Andrew nodded and shoved his wallet back into his jeans. He'd heard that phrase bandied about. He shouldn't ever be thanked for his service. He'd failed his men.

When he cleared the door, he palmed his phone and called Jose's cell.

"Hello?" Jose's wife Corrie answered the phone.

"Hi, Corrie. We made it in. Do you need any help today?"

"Hi, Cap. No, actually, I think everything is done. There is a coordinator here at the VA that has walked me through claiming my survivor benefits and handling the funeral arrangements. I've done a lot of paperwork since Jose died. Stupid, I knew he was dying, I just couldn't bring myself to look at what had to be done. I wasn't ready for it."

"Nobody was." He leaned against the rental car and drew a shaky breath. "I can come over if there is anything you'd like me to do."

"That's so sweet. Thank you, but until tomorrow's over, I'm going to push all the paperwork to the side. My plans for tonight include taking one of the sleeping pills the doctors gave me and turning in early. I'm sorry, I'm not much of a hostess."

"You aren't supposed to entertain me. I'm here for you."

"Then please be there tomorrow. It's going to be hard." She whispered the words, and he could hear her tears in that small request.

More of those inappropriate feelings flashed forward. He gritted his teeth and batted them back. "I'll be there. Good night, Corrie."

"Good night, Cap."

Drew stared at the bag holding his service dress uniform. He'd postponed getting dressed as long as he could. Gen was ready and waiting for him. He had to put the damn thing on. "Get over yourself." With a yank, he pulled the zipper down. He reached into the bottom of the bag and removed his wheel hat. He took the cover off and used a washcloth from the hotel's bathroom to wipe off the dust from the brim. He pulled out his dress shoes and did the same. There were two pairs of slacks to wear with the uniform, blue for winter and white for summer. He removed the white from the hanger and stepped into them. He tucked in his T-shirt and continued to get dressed, stepping into his shoes and tying them in a double-knot. He'd donned this uniform for formal and semi-formal events, parades, and ceremonies. He wished like hell he could skip this ceremony, however. He buttoned the jacket and made sure his belt was straight before he allowed himself to look in the mirror. He'd gained bulk and weight being back at the ranch. The fit was tight, but it would do for today. He reached for his hat and the blue box that held the last medal he was awarded.

It took three full breaths before he opened the door. Gen turned, her long hair pulled back in an updo. The black dress she wore was simple: sleeveless and perfect. She stood up, taller in her heels. "You look amazing." She stepped forward and touched his medals then lifted her finger to his collar where his rank was displayed. "Are you ready to go?"

"No." He handed her the medal. "I need to put this on.

She looked at the box and then at him before

opening it. "My goodness. It's big."

Drew snorted. "Ostentatious. It hangs around my neck. Would you, please?" He picked up the medal that was suspended by a light blue ribbon and turned around.

"How do you... oh, got it." He could feel her fiddling with the ribbon. "There." He let go of the medal and glanced at the mirrored closet doors. "What medal is that?"

"CMOH." He shrugged, trying to play it off.

"What does that stand for?"

"The Congressional Medal of Honor."

She blinked up at him. "It's important, isn't it?"

He nodded. "Yeah."

"What did you get it for?"

He drew a breath. "For my actions after the IED exploded. I don't deserve it, Gen. I didn't do anything that anyone else in my position wouldn't have done."

She put both her hands on his face and looked up into his eyes. "I have a feeling they don't hand those medals out to just anyone, am I right?" He tried to give her a smile and wasn't too sure he was successful. "I will tell you this until you believe it. You are an amazing man, one who took care of the men in his command the best he could. You're hurting because some of your men didn't make it. It's okay to feel what you feel. But if they gave you this medal, someone saw something that you're not looking at, and I suspect it was the totality of your actions that day."

He broke eye contact with her and moved to pick up his hat. "It doesn't bring anyone back."

"It doesn't. You can't bring them back, Drew. And because no one except God could, you owe it to each of them to live your life to the fullest, be everything they knew and trusted you to be. Gunny loved you, Barry needed you, and those other men believed in you and what they were fighting for. Be that man." He turned around and stared at her. She walked to him and kissed his cheek. "It sucks to bear that much expectation, but if Gunny didn't think you could handle it, he would have cut his losses. Am I right, Marine?"

His eyes shone with unshed tears as he smiled. "Yes, ma'am, you are correct." He lowered his head and kissed her gently. "Is it wrong to be happy to have you in my life? How can I be happy when Gunny just died?" He stared at the woman he loved. There wasn't any trumpet or fanfare at the revelation, just a deep, quiet peace that filled him.

She shook her head and placed a hand on each shoulder. "Drew, Gunny is gone. You will always love and cherish the memories he gave you, and if I know you, you will impart all his wisdom to the people throughout Hollister. It is all right to keep living. Gunny had his destiny, and you have yours. Would he want you to die with him? What would he say to you if he heard that type of talk?"

Andrew lifted his face to the ceiling and drew a deep shaking breath before he looked at her, "I believe he would say, 'Captain, are you fucking insane? Have I taught you nothing? Screw your head on straight, quit crying like a girl, and show up.'"

She laughed and kissed him gently. "Then screw your head on straight, Captain. Let's go pay our respects to Gunny and his wife. Then we have a life to live."

He nodded and grabbed his hat and keys. Gen took his arm and he escorted her to the vehicle, opened the door for her, and waited until she was seat-belted in before he shut the door and got into the driver's side.

It took fifteen minutes to make it to the church. He pulled up and stared at the Marine Honor Guard. "Damn it." This funeral wasn't supposed to be about him.

"What's wrong?" Gen reached over and put her hand on his leg.

"Nothing. Could you help me with this?" He handed her a white glove, and together, they stretched it over the cast on his left wrist. She slid the other one on.

"Okay. Ready?"

"No, but we better go anyway." He exited the SUV and went around to help her out of the vehicle and escort her to the church.

The sergeant-in-charge of the Honor Guard saw him and immediately snapped to attention, shouting, "Honor Guard, A-ten shun!" In unison, the seven riflemen, four color guards, and the sergeant snapped to attention. "Present arms!" The command was followed, and the enlisted Honor Guard held their salute. He returned their salute and walked into the chapel.

Andrew took off his wheel cap and put it under his arm. They walked through the narthex. The sergeant hustled ahead of them, opened the door, and once again called the building to attention. Upon Drew's entrance, every military member in attendance turned in unison and faced him. "Present arms." The members saluted. Andrew returned the salute and moved Gen down the aisle. He saw Corrie and made a direct line to her. When he arrived, he pulled the woman into his arms and held her.

"Corrie, I am so sorry." He held her and rocked her back and forth.

"Oh, Cap, he loved you so much. You were his officer. He raised you from a snot-nosed lieutenant. I know he is on the other side, wanting to slug your arm and tell you to stop crying!"

Drew laughed at her remark and let her go. "He'd never let me forget he raised me." He looked to Corrie's left and froze. The tall, broad man standing beside Corrie stared back at Drew. The man's body was ramrod straight and tense before he extended his hand. "Captain, good to see you again."

"Barry? Barry Marks? My God! They told me... They said you wouldn't recover." Andrew's astonishment did not stop him from pulling the man into his arms and hugging him like he was a long-lost brother.

Barry whapped his back a couple times and then

they parted. Barry pulled away and cleared his throat. "It's been a slow process, Captain. Gunny got me released, and he and Corrie applied some tough love. I still have… you know… dreams and some… well, a lot of anger and control issues, but I am doing better."

"Damn. I'm so happy for you." Andrew pulled Gen close and introduced her. "Corrie and Barry, this is Genevieve Wheeler. Gen, this is Gunny Sanchez's wife Corrine, or Corrie as we call her. And this is Barry Marks."

Gen nodded at the young man. "I've heard so much about you, Barry, I'm glad to meet you." She turned to the widow and touched her arm. "Corrie, I am so sorry for your loss."

Corrie's blue-grey eyes glistened, and she nodded, "My Jose had a lot of demons. He fought as long and as hard as he could, but in the end, he was just too tired to fight anymore. The pain from the bone cancer was unbearable and the medication they gave him in the end couldn't control it. He took matters into his own hands like he always did. If this cancer hadn't eaten him alive, he would have been here right now, yelling at all of us to screw our heads on straight, stop crying, and show up."

Gen smiled sadly and looked at Andrew. "Boy, did you peg that one." Drew's eyes glistened with restrained tears as he nodded his head once solemnly. The battle to control his emotions seemed to take all his focus and energy, and Gen got it. She squeezed his hand gently.

Corrie smiled and patted Andrew's arm. "Come on, Captain, you and Gen are sitting up here with Barry and me. The Corps told me we have a two-star general coming today, and I want a front-row seat when he realizes he has a Congressional Medal of Honor recipient here that he needs to honor. You know that would make Jose laugh like a loon. That weird sense of humor of his."

Drew escorted the ladies to the pew. He sat by Gen and Barry sat with Corrie. He found himself glancing over at FNG. The kid looked good. *Kid*. Hell, after what he'd been through, he wasn't a kid even though he wasn't probably twenty-five yet.

Drew sat still as the funeral started. The military funeral was run efficiently and professionally. Gunnery Sergeant Jose Sanchez served the Corps honorably, was medically retired although he had his twenty in, and the man was a highly decorated war hero. The Marine Corps paid him the respect he deserved. After the chaplain finished the service, Drew, Barry, and four other Marines he didn't know acted as pallbearers and loaded Gunny's casket into the hearse. He met Gen at their vehicle, and they pulled into the long line of cars following the hearse and family limo.

He walked slowly across the grass, giving Gen his arm. There were four chairs. Corrie motioned for them to move forward. He helped Gen into her seat and then sat down, staring at the hole in the ground. The dark earth mounded under a blue cloth as if it could hide the inevitability of that ground covering the casket. The chaplain led a prayer, and then the flag was removed from the casket. The Honor Guard performed a twenty-one-gun salute and the flag was folded and presented to Corrie. She nodded and accepted the flag. The coffin was lowered, and the chaplain invited Corrie to where he was standing.

She handed the flag to Gen and stood. Corrie Sanchez was a stalwart of strength until she bent over and grabbed a handful of dirt. A chill ran down Drew's spine as the eerie sound of Taps being played by a lone trumpet echoed over the gravestones that surrounded them. Corrie froze, unmoving and unresponsive to the chaplain's whispered words. The haunting melody crippled Corrie as she stood, weeping silently at the gravesite.

Drew stood and walked forward, wrapping his arms around the woman. He held her, his voice a low rumble as he whispered in her ear, "You can do this. You're going to make it, we'll both make it, together. Walk with me." She nodded slowly, still weeping. He helped her back to her seat and took his place behind her, standing ramrod straight with a hand on her shoulder as the funeral continued. He glanced at the man sitting next to Corrie. Barry's face appeared to be etched in stone. No emotion. Gen reached over and held Corrie's hand until the end of the ceremony. They stood with Corrie as people he didn't know extended their condolences. Corrie nodded and thanked them, but he doubted she saw anyone or would ever remember what was said.

Corrie turned toward the gravesite. Andrew asked, "Do you want any time alone with him?"

She shook her head. "We said our goodbyes many times in the last two years. I wasn't ready. He was." She turned and looked at him. "Walk with us to our car?"

"Of course." Gen was the one that answered. The women walked together ahead of him and Barry.

He glanced at the young man. "How are you?"

Barry looked up at him. "Not good."

"Do you have someone to talk to?" He assumed the guy was getting treatment.

"Corrie. We'll be fine. I'll keep it under control." Barry left him and made his way to the limo, opening the door for Corrie.

Corrie stopped. "Go ahead and get in, Barry. I'll be right there." Barry nodded and slid into the car, leaving the door open. "Captain, Jose left an envelope for you. I was going to just mail it to you, but would you and Gen like to come by tomorrow night and have a drink and dinner with Barry and me? I know Jose would have wanted us to have a stiff belt and a good visit after such a bitch of a day."

Drew looked at Gen, and she nodded as she squeezed his fingers. He turned and smiled sadly.

"What is your address? We'll stop and get something for dinner on the way over."

Corrie shook her head. "Oh, Lord above. No. Please don't bring any more food! Barry and I will be eating leftovers for a month as it is. The staff at the VA and the hospice workers have been so nice. Please, just change out of that monkey suit—Jose's words, not mine—and come over. We are in temporary lodging at the VA in Reno. Just ask the gate guard and he will give you directions. See you at about six?"

Drew nodded and bent to kiss her on the cheek and whispered, "We will be there. Will you be all right alone with Barry?"

She hugged him and patted his shoulder as he straightened. "I will be fine. That young man is the son Jose and I were never able to have. He has handled this better than I expected, but I'll watch him closely. I know what to do if he has problems. He'd never hurt me."

Drew walked her to the car and helped her in. He waited until she was settled before he shut the door and rapped the top with his knuckles. The driver pulled away slowly from the curb.

Gen stepped in front of him, her hands running up his dark blue sleeves to his shoulders. "Everyone has left the gravesite. Do you want to go back and say your goodbyes?"

Closing his eyes, he filled his lungs with air and nodded. "Yeah, I need to… yeah."

"Good, I will go to the SUV and wait. You take as long as you need." She leaned up to kiss him. Before their lips met, he enfolded her to him tightly. She melted into him and held him as tightly as he was holding her. Their soft, searching, tender kiss held them closer together than any of his physical strength could. Drew pulled away slowly and he gazed at her. No words were exchanged. The raw emotion that passed between them would only be cheapened by words. He bent down and kissed her forehead before he slowly released her and stepped away. Turning, he straightened his back and resolutely walked to the gravesite.

Drew stood in front of the gaping hole in the ground and looked at the coffin. Lifting his head, he shrugged his shoulders, trying to loosen the pain in his chest. It didn't work. The pain was unlike any he'd ever suffered. He cast a tear-filled gaze around the area. A fat tear fell unabated. He stared at the coffin and let his anger out. "Damn it, Jose. I can't believe you ate a bullet, man. I am fucking mad at you, you asshole. I'm so mad. You ripped us off. I was coming. I was going to say goodbye. Hell, I talked to you three days before you did this. You said nothing. I would have come then. You know I would have." He heaved a sob and shook his head. The tears fell, and he didn't fucking care who saw him cry. He shook his head. "Yeah, I know you were hurting, God knows I understand how bad the pain can be, but... you left Corrie and Barry and me.

I'm so mad! How could you, man? How could you leave us? Fuck, Gunny, why did you do it?" His white-gloved hand swiped at the tears that fell down his cheek. "Damn it, Jose, don't you know I loved you, man? I never told you, but I did. You had to have known that. I wanted to tell you. You didn't give me the chance."

Drew paced the eight feet to the foot of Jose's gravesite and then did an about-face and came back. Looking around and seeing absolutely nothing but that gaping hole in the ground, he shook his head and continued, "Not sure how to say goodbye here, Gunny. Actually, I have no fucking clue how to do it." He watched several people walk past, going to a headstone about fifty feet away. "Gen and I are going to have dinner with Corrie and Barry tomorrow." He sniffed and wiped his face again. "Fuck, yeah, I know. Stop crying and show up. Well, I never cried before, Gunny. You ruined that. I cried the day I found out you were gone, and I cried today. I'm not going to apologize for that. But I showed up, man. So, deal with it."

He paced back and forth for a couple minutes. "I brought someone with me. Her name is Gen. She's special. Damn, you would have loved her. She is squared away. Tight. Tight enough to keep me centered, and we all know I'm seriously fucked up. Shit, man, I'm falling in love with her. Probably way too soon for that to be thrown out there, so we'll keep it between us for now." Andrew's laugh was more of a sob. He glanced over at the rental SUV and smiled sadly. "Damn it to hell, Gunny, I wish you could have met her. Because she's in my life, I have a pretty damn good clue what is in that letter you left for me. Don't you worry—I got your six, man. I'll take care of both of them. Corrie and Barry. I'll make sure they're okay." A tear slowly trickled down his face. This time, he didn't bother to wipe it away.

Once again, he looked toward the woman sitting patiently, waiting for him. "She told me you would be proud of me, doing what you taught me... taking care of my people. If she will let me, I will take care of her until I draw my last breath."

He dropped his head and pulled in a ragged lungful of air, fighting to staunch the emotions, and yeah, the fucking tears. "I'm sorry I yelled at you, man. I'm sorry I'm mad at you. I'm going to miss you, Jose." He stood straight and drew in several long breaths, gathering the strength to do what he needed to do. "I think it's time to screw my head on straight, stop crying, and show up now, my man, or you may come back to haunt me. God knows I don't need any more ghosts."

Drew took three steps toward the SUV. He hesitated, turned back, and snapped to attention. Captain Andrew Hollister, Congressional Medal of Honor Recipient, lifted his white-gloved hand in a solemn salute to his fellow Marine—and his friend. "Semper Fi, Gunny. Rest in peace, your watch is over. You are relieved of duty; I'll take it from here." He slowly lowered his hand, did an about-face, and walked away.

CHAPTER 17

Emotionally drained silence reigned on the ride back to the hotel. The poignant canyon of emotions had emptied both of them. Gen understood the day had devastated him, forcing him to examine memories he would rather never see again. She sat on the couch and watched as he put his uniform away. Wearing only his boxer shorts, his ripped body was phenomenal to watch as he methodically prepared the uniform for travel.

Quietly, she stood and slid out of the black sheath she had worn to the funeral. The shoes and underwear fell next to the black material on the ground. Gen walked quietly behind him and slid her hands up his bare back. He straightened, his muscles rippling under her touch. Gen leaned forward and kissed his shoulder, wrapping her hands around his waist and pulling him back into her bare body. His body's reaction was immediate. A hiss of drawn air, the tensing of his muscles, and the almost-instantaneous turn of his body in her arms.

Gen's hands traveled to his waist, pushing the elastic band of his boxers down over his growing erection and hips. Her hands lifted and moved against his body. Slowly cupping his shaft, the hot, soft skin felt silky and smooth against her hand, yet his size and hardness yielded nothing as she caressed him. The sensation of his lips on her throat and his fingers on her breast sent rivulets of desire through her. He growled deeply and picked her up, carrying her to the bed.

Drew lowered his body on top of hers. She felt his warmth from her shins to her shoulders. Her breasts took his weight as he lowered himself closer to her. The desire to be with him, to have him deep inside of her body, reverberated in every fiber of her being. The taste and smell of him intoxicated her senses, and her only coherent thought was to possess every part of him so completely he would become a part of her.

Gen let her hands and lips travel over every inch of his body. His hand traveled over her stomach toward her sex. She moaned and arched her back, wanting more than the tease of the fingering of her folds. Drew understood, and his lips moved lower. Her hands slipped through the short cut of his hair, no longer able to tangle her fingers in the thickness. It didn't matter;

she grabbed the bedspread and fisted it as he spread her legs, making room for his shoulders.

She lifted to watch and moaned as he licked her. Drew lifted his attention to her. His gaze held hers as he kissed the inside of her thigh. His deep voice rumbled, punctuated by his soft kisses of her thighs. "God, I need you."

Gen's eyes held his, and she was mesmerized by the desire she saw in his gaze. He lowered his head but not those eyes. His fingers spread her open, and she jolted away from him when his tongue caressed her. "Oh, baby, you are so hot and wet." He kissed her and licked the sensitive skin. His good arm wrapped around her leg and over her hip, anchoring her down on the bed. He stopped and kissed her inner thigh, "You are so sweet, babe. I love the way you taste." His mouth lowered again, his tongue and lips carefully working her sensitive flesh. He took his time, teasing and exploring before he took her clit into his mouth. Unable to stop the movement, her body stiffened and bucked against his assault. When she settled after crashing through her orgasm, he kissed her inner thighs and moved back up her body.

Lowering himself onto her, he claimed her mouth. The kiss was more than a physical thing. The way he held her, touched her, gazed at her—everything told her it was more. Lifting himself, he centered over her and thrust forward, moving into her slowly.

Gen allowed herself to admit what she felt for this

man. As he made love to her, she felt like her body was on fire from the inside. The physical sensations coupled with an emotional discovery that she couldn't deny. They were lost in each other, and she felt as if they were one as he worked his cock deep into her. It didn't take long for him to find the rhythm they needed. Sliding his arms under her, he lifted her body into his embrace, holding her tight against his chest. The change of angle allowed him to go deeper. Her sex once again clenched, shattering her as she tumbled into her orgasm. Black spots painted her vision as Drew lost control and pounded through his climax.

She cradled him as he recovered. Drew laid his head in the crook of her neck, and he brushed a soft kiss across her shoulder. Her arms clung to his body, her hands grasping onto his back. Their shared perspiration made his skin slick as he moved back to kiss her swollen lips. His eyes were hooded as she searched them. She knew she was rushing it, but she couldn't help feeling an overwhelming love for this man.

He smiled slowly and lowered to kiss her. With his lips against hers, he whispered, "Baby, I'm falling in love with you."

She gasped, his kiss preventing her from saying anything. She let him lead and kissed him back as his tongue searched for hers. When he lifted away, Gen stared up at him. "I feel the same thing. Are we crazy?"

Andrew smiled. "Probably, but I kind of like where I'm at."

"Then crazy it is because I'm not going anywhere."

He laid down on his side and pulled her closer. "Thank you for today."

She let her fingers play with his chest hairs. "I didn't do anything."

"You did. You propped me up. If you hadn't come, I probably wouldn't have either. I needed this. I needed the closure. Thank you for supporting me through it."

"I wouldn't be anywhere else." She tipped her head back and kissed his chin. "I'll be here as long as you need me."

"Can you fit forever into your schedule?" Andrew chuckled as he asked the question, but Gen heard the insecurity. They'd both had people in their life that had cheated on them. They both knew that pain.

She bent back so she could see him. "I can for you. You and me."

"You and me." He nodded. "No one else."

"Never. We've both experienced those types of people. We aren't them. You and me. Together. No one else. I promise." She stared at him as he searched her eyes.

"I promise." He repeated the words and lowered his lips.

Corrie poured a shot of tequila into each glass and handed them out to the somber gathering. She raised hers and took a deep breath. "Jose, we loved you, and we will miss you. Semper Fi."

Gen tipped her small shot glass up and chugged it. She coughed and turned red as the alcohol burned down her throat. Drew's arm pulled her close as he laughed. "Not a tequila girl?"

She coughed again and shook her head. "Ahhh… no, I am more of the whiskey type." Drew took the glass from her hand and placed it on the table.

Corrie smiled understandingly. "Honestly, I never acquired a taste for tequila either, but Jose liked this rotgut." Corrie put the shot glasses back onto the tray. Barry lifted the tray with the glasses and tequila and took it into the small kitchen without saying a word.

Andrew nodded his head toward Barry and whispered, "How is everything?"

Corrie drew a deep breath. "We're good. But we are in a weird place right now. It is hard to try to focus on the future. Since we found out about Jose's bone cancer, we've lived each day for that day. Making plans on what to do for the rest of our lives is… huge." Her slim legs tucked gracefully up under her. She curled into the arm of the couch and chuckled. "I haven't worked in years." She looked at Gen and explained, "I left my job because Jose didn't want me to work. Once he made gunnery sergeant, I became a full-time wife and I loved it." Barry sat down on the opposite end of the couch, his large body taking up most of the small structure. Corrie smiled at him and continued, "Then, when Barry was released, I was blessed with his strength and help. Jose was a prideful and obstinate man, but he allowed Barry to help him. When the cancer got bad, Barry was able to lift him and help me with his day-to-day needs."

Barry closed his eyes as if the memories were too strong. Drew cleared his throat and leaned forward. "Corrie, I want you and Barry to come live with me in South Dakota." At her startled look, he held up a hand and continued. "I have a very good life in Hollister. I will set you up in a small house in town if you don't want to stay at the ranch. If you don't like it, consider it a transition location until you both know what you want to do. No pressure and no expectations, just a safe harbor until you heal."

Barry's vivid blue eyes locked onto Corrie, waiting for her to speak. Her eyes blinked rapidly as if trying to comprehend what he'd just said. Finally, she smiled politely. "Thank you, Captain, but you don't have to do this."

Andrew puffed out his cheeks and blew out a breath. "Yeah, I know I don't, but I want to. You need time to figure out what you want to do with the rest of your life. Hollister is a good place to do just that." Drew reached over and took Gen's hand before he continued, "You don't have to decide right now. The offer stands today, next week, or next year."

Gen squeezed his hand and ran her free hand up his forearm. "It really is a great place to find your center."

Drew stood up and looked over at Barry. "Hey, man, I need to stretch my legs. Want to show me this yard?"

Barry stood and headed out of the small quarters. As soon as they were out of the house, Barry turned to him. "You don't have to stretch your legs. The question is what do you really want?"

"How are you doing? Emotionally, how are you handling this?" Drew walked beside him.

"With silence. I keep words unsaid and my anger funneled inwards."

"Are you mad, too?" Drew asked. "I am. I'm so mad at him. I have been since he died."

Barry stopped and turned toward him. "Died? Fuck, he didn't die, the rat bastard killed himself. I was ten minutes away to take Corrie to an appointment, ten minutes. Mad? No, I'm fucking furious with him. How could he leave without saying goodbye? He was everything, man. Father, brother, friend, and confidant. Damn it to hell, what am I going to do now? How in the hell am I going to survive? And yes, I'm being a selfish son of a bitch. I should be worrying about Corrie and making sure she's okay, but my fucking problems keep shoving to the surface. I'm a fucking mess."

Drew glanced over at the man walking beside him. Barry was exactly where Drew had been at the gravesite yesterday. "That's pretty much word for word what I said to him yesterday after everyone left the graveyard. At least we know where we stand. It's a starting point. I have someone I talk to once a week. Just started, but it seems to help. Do you have anyone?"

"Jose, and now Corrie." Barry shrugged.

"I meant a professional," Drew clarified.

"I know what you meant. I don't, and I don't want one. I've had enough of shrinks."

They continued to stroll through the big yard. Drew changed subjects. "Barry, how is Corrie really doing? Is she putting on a front, or is she really okay?" Drew picked up a stick from the sidewalk and started breaking it into pieces as they walked.

"She is strong. I think she was the only one who wasn't surprised Jose ate a bullet." Barry nodded across the street.

Following his lead, Drew stepped off the curb and headed toward the main road. "I meant what I said about coming to South Dakota. I can always use a hand on the ranch, but if you don't want to work for me, hell, there are other options."

Barry said nothing for a moment and then asked, "What did you do to your arm?"

Drew held up the cast and sneered. "Gen's ex-fiancé got a case of the batshit crazies. I stepped in against a home run swing from a Louisville Slugger."

"You win?" Barry's blue eyes were flint-hard.

"Always. One right and the mother was down and out," Drew chuckled dryly.

Barry grunted. "That's you, Cap. Cocky and self-assured. I remember it, you know. Everything. I remember you bleeding and torn to hell but holding off superior forces. It was almost like you were possessed, fighting through the night, moving your ass and making each shot count. You kept going even when you should have been passed out from blood loss. Shit, Gunny had passed out. Pip was in a heap on the bottom of the trench they were in, and me? Well, you know what happened to me. I was frozen, I physically couldn't move. The stench of the blood, the heat and the pain. Yeah, I remember everything. Every. Fucking. Thing. Especially what I didn't do. Fight."

Drew stopped and waited for the man beside him to look at him. It took several minutes, but he did. "There is a clinical diagnosis for what happened to you. You are not a failure. Your mind couldn't process the hell you were living through. I'd have you on my team any fucking day and twice on Sunday. Do you hear me, Marine? You are a damn good man."

Barry looked away. Drew hoped like hell he'd said the right words. Knowing that what happened wasn't his fault might help Barry deal with what he'd lived through. He drew a deep breath. Look at him playing shrink. Wouldn't Jeremiah be proud?

Finally, Barry started walking again, and Drew fell

into step. "Captain, if she'll go, I'll get Corrie out there to you. It would be good for her to be around folks that can take care of her."

Drew nodded. A positive step in the right direction, but he needed to make sure Barry stuck around, too. He'd promised to watch out for both of them. "You have done a good job with that so far. Will you come?"

"Smalltown, USA, isn't for me, sir." Barry led him down a pine tree-lined street that hedged the Veterans Administration campus. "Besides, you don't want me there."

Drew tossed the last of the branch he'd snapped into pieces out of his hands. "Really? Why's that?"

"Because if I lose it, I could kill someone, someone you may care about." Barry shrugged. "I'm dangerous."

Drew gave him a sideways glance. "Yeah? So the fuck am I, Marine. What makes you more dangerous than me?"

Barry stopped and looked over the massive lawn in front of the administration building. "You have a reason to keep it under control. I don't."

Drew put his hand on his hip and cocked his head, staring at the man. "Yeah, you do, you just haven't realized it yet."

Corrie handed Gen another glass of wine as they put the casserole in the oven. "May I ask you a personal question, Gen?"

Gen lifted her eyes from the bread she had been coating with butter and smiled. "Sure."

"How long have you known the captain?"

"Not long. Why?"

"He loves you. You know that right?" Corrie handed her the shredded parmesan cheese.

Taking the dish, Gen smiled and blushed. "Ahh yeah, we kind of confirmed that last night... and this morning."

Corrie laughed gleefully. "Oh! That is way too much information!"

"Well, you did ask!" Gen laughed as her face warmed from the blush that slammed over her cheeks.

Corrie's laughter subsided and her face softened. "You hang on to that man. Nothing in this world is more important than love. Jose and I had a love like that once."

Gen set the cheese down and put her hand over Corrie's. "Once?"

Corrie's eyes glazed over. "Before he was injured and diagnosed. Since then, he wouldn't touch me. Damn man thought I couldn't be attracted to him." Corrie wiped impatiently at the tears that ran down her cheeks. "Then the chemo and medicines made him so sick." She smiled and shrugged. "Don't get me wrong, I loved him. He was my world, but I have been lonely for a long time."

"Then come back to South Dakota with us. Start fresh. Look, I have a small diner, and I need full-time help. It is busier than I can handle on my own. I don't know what the pay would be yet, but I know you would be helping me, and I know I want to have the ability to take time off to be with Drew. With him at the ranch and me in town, it is… difficult."

The older woman wiped down the counter and shook her head. "I don't have any experience in a restaurant. I was a secretary for the Corps when I met and married Jose. You'd be better off hiring someone who knows the business."

"Oh, well, in that case, I should probably fire myself. I had no experience when I opened the place. I just committed to making a few things well and keeping the prices reasonable. The idea worked. Too well, it would seem. When we came here, I closed up shop. I'm sure I'll hear all about that when I get home. I have some regulars that have forgotten how to cook or make coffee for themselves."

Corrie's laughter was soft but genuine. "I like you, Gen. If you are serious about the offer, I'll come work for you." Looking around the small quarters they'd been given, Corrie took a deep breath. "Barry will need to be convinced to stay with me. He needs an anchor, and I need my boy." Turning to Gen, she smiled. "I am only twelve years older than he is, but he is my son as sure as I gave birth to him. His folks are dead, and Jose and I adopted him."

"He'll be welcome. You'll learn to love Hollister. It's a town that wraps itself around you, and you'll never want to leave." Gen smiled and glanced out the window, seeing the two men returning to the little apartment. "You and me forever," she whispered to herself.

CHAPTER 18

The alarm clock's shrill silenced immediately after Gen slapped the top of the abominable machine. Groaning, she turned and snuggled close to him. He'd only slept a couple hours. His time awake before her alarm went off had been spent in contemplation. Her breathing evened out, and she stilled. He rubbed her arm. "No, ma'am, up and at 'em. You have customers coming and I have a ranch waiting."

Gen grumbled something unintelligible and burrowed closer. They'd gotten in at midnight. Four hours wasn't enough sleep. "Can't we pretend we are still gone?" Her words were muffled because she'd cuddled so close.

Drew stroked her hair and sighed, "Unfortunately, I need to check in with Senior and Ryan and you need to find out if anyone died from starvation. True?" A noncommittal noise and lowering hands forced a laugh from him. "Don't start something we don't have time to finish, Gen."

Her face tilted up to his, the mischief in her eyes plainly visible. "So the foreman of your ranch and cows wait ten or fifteen minutes and the customers only have one urn of coffee perked." Lifting up on her elbow, her dark hair draped over her shoulders and breasts. "Make love to me, Drew. I need to know what we had in Nevada was real."

He pulled her down to him and searched her face. "I love you, Genevieve. I know it is too fast and I know that is freaking both of us out a bit, but what I feel is real." The deep timbre of his voice vibrated under her.

Her finger traced his lips. "I'm scared at how fast this happened, but I am certain of what I feel." As she lowered to kiss him, her alarm shrilled again. Rolling away, she slapped the offending box and flipped the toggle, turning the alarm off.

Drew pulled her back to him. "I want to take you out to the ranch tonight for dinner. I want you to meet my dad."

Gen's eyes popped and she squeaked, "Tonight? Wait, I've met your dad several times. He's come into the diner before."

His laughter filled the room. "Yes, tonight. You haven't met him as my lover."

"Good God. You aren't going to introduce me like that, are you?" Drew laughed and waggled his eyebrows. Gen narrowed her eyes and lifted a finger. "You—"

"I wouldn't. Girlfriend?"

She relaxed in his arms. "That's better. Wait! What should I wear? Should I bring something? I will bring a pie or a cake. Or shouldn't I?"

Cupping her face in his hands, he kissed her, stopping her minor freak-out. "Gen, we have a cook at the ranch. Bring dessert but only if you want to. Wear jeans, and I would love it if you wore the boots with heels. They're sexy."

Her eyes widened. "Sexy? To meet your dad? Shouldn't I be dowdy or conservative or something?"

"No, I want him to see the woman I love. Be yourself. I'll pick you up at six. Now, go get ready for work, my love."

Her face broke into a huge smile. "Your love? I am, aren't I?"

He laughed again and kissed her nose. "You are. Now go!"

Giggling, she bounded into the bathroom and turned on the shower. Drew continued to smile as she sang horribly off-key while she got ready. The vitality and energy she had from the night's sleep escaped him. He'd managed maybe two hours, but he had a mission today.

Andrew pulled his truck up and drew a bracing breath into his lungs. This confrontation should have happened long ago. Call him a chickenshit, but until now, he just wasn't willing to deal with it. He walked into the big ranch house that he'd grown up in. His great-great-great-grandfather had built the back portion. The entire structure held a family of six. It was now the kitchen and had been remodeled and insulated to be warm and cheery. That was where he found his father, talking with Clara, their cook.

His father looked up when he entered and immediately stopped laughing. Drew straightened. "Sir, I'd like to speak with you."

His father nodded and got up. "The office. Clara, would you bring us some coffee, please?"

"Sure. Just give me a second," the woman spoke to them from the sink where she was washing breakfast plates.

Andrew stepped aside and let his father lead the way. The creak of the old wooden floors was the same as it always had been, but today, Andrew sensed the history that had walked the boards. This was the newer part of the house although you couldn't tell any longer where the additions started and ended. His father had remodeled extensively after Andrew's mother had died.

"Have a seat."

"Thank you." He sat down and crossed his ankle over his knee.

"So, I expect you'll be telling me you're leaving." Senior leaned back. The man looked tired and old.

Andrew cocked his head. "No. Do you want me to leave?" His defenses lifted and his gut clenched.

"What? No. I just figured you'd be leaving."

"Why?"

Clara kicked the door open. "Here we are, coffee, and I brought a couple of the cinnamon sugar biscuits. Andrew, I put sugar on the tray, too. I know you like your coffee sweet. Can I get you anything else?"

"No, thank you, Clara," Senior answered for them. Andrew gave the woman a quick smile. Ryan's wife was a wonder and had been keeping house for Senior for as long as he could remember.

Drew waited until Clara shut the door behind her before he leaned in and grabbed a mug and dosed it with sugar. "You were telling me why you thought I was leaving?"

"You hate it here." Senior leaned forward and grasped the other mug.

"I don't." Andrew took a sip of his coffee. The ranch had always been a solace to him.

"Then you hate me." His father stated the fact and stared straight at him.

Andrew set his mug down on his leg and drew a breath. He'd practiced this conversation in his head for years. Now that it was time, the words he'd wanted to use like a sword seemed... wrong. He stared at the sole of his cowboy boot and began. "As long as I can remember, I've never done anything good enough for you, Senior. No matter how hard I tried, I was inadequate. I could have done it better, or I should have done it another way. I know you don't approve of me, what I've done, or who I grew up to be. I can't help that. I learned that lesson. I also know that I'm not the person you want me to be. I'm a disappointment to you." He shrugged and continued before his father could speak. "I don't hate you, sir, but for as long as I can remember, you've hated me. As a matter of fact, I can't ever remember you telling me that you were proud of me or that you loved me. My entire life." He picked up his coffee cup and shrugged. "But growing up and going to war teaches a man a thing or two. I can't change the fact that I'm a disappointment to you. All I can do is be the best man I can be. If it isn't good enough, then…" He shrugged. "I won't apologize for being who I am."

Senior sat silent, staring at his coffee cup. He swallowed hard and put the cup on his desk. "I was lost after your mom died. I didn't know how to raise you." He straightened and stared at Drew. "I did the best I could. My old man raised me the way I raised you. I wanted you to be strong. Didn't know how to tell you the stuff your mom should have told you." Senior's brows burrowed. "Know I didn't say it but hoped you'd know it. All of this, everything we built, is for you and yours. Thought you were going to tell me you were leaving again."

"No. I came to get this out in the open." He lifted his coffee and took a sip.

"Why?" Senior asked the question while fiddling with the handle of his mug.

"Clear the air. I've got a lot of baggage from my time overseas. This doesn't need to be weighing me down."

"The dreams, that the baggage you're talking about?" His father took a sip of his coffee.

"Yes. I've started seeing someone to help me get through that." He wanted his father to know although he was almost positive his father would consider him weak for not being able to sort it out himself.

Senior nodded and took a sip of his coffee. "I apologize for not being man enough to say the words. I'm proud of who you've become, and I love you." His father's eyes filled with tears. "Thought I'd never get to say that to you when I got the call from the Marines. Knew you wouldn't want to come home again after that woman cheated on you and everyone knew."

Andrew blinked, trying to follow the conversation. "Stephanie? Dad, I never loved her. I asked her to marry me because it was what everyone expected. You, especially."

His father's eyebrows raised. "Me?"

"How many times did you ask me if I was going to marry her?" Andrew chuckled. "At least once a day."

Senior shifted in his chair. "Didn't mean to force

you, just wanted you to be happy like I was with your mom."

Andrew nodded. "I am now."

Senior's head snapped up. "With the Wheeler woman?"

"Yes. We've been dating for a while now. She went with me to the funeral in Nevada."

"She have that situation with the slicker fixed? The one that took a bat to you and threatened to sue you?"

"As far as I know. Has he dropped any more threats?" Andrew took a gulp of his coffee now that it was cool enough to drink.

"Haven't heard anything else. My lawyers were going to slap back with a counter-suit based on that video of Ken's. He drove out and showed me what his dashcam picked up. Got a copy of it for my lawyer. Entirely too much damn paperwork, but I went ahead and did it legal. Good right hook, by the way."

Andrew blinked. That was the first time his father had ever told him he measured up. He kind of liked the feeling. "Thanks. Dude went down hard."

"Did you hear the Marshalls lost a big portion of their home due to a gas leak in the house?"

"Propane? Must have been a big tank."

"That's what Frank said." Senior leveled a smirking gaze at him. "Bullshit if you ask me, but no one asked me. Frank wanted to make sure you knew he appreciated all your help."

Andrew nodded. "Neighborly thing to do."

"Are you going to tell me what you know?" Senior took a good swallow of his coffee and reached over, pushing the biscuits in Drew's direction. "Had one of these for breakfast. They're good."

Andrew grabbed one. "Thank you. You don't want to know what I know."

"Why's that?"

"Classified. If I told you, I'd have to kill you, and seeing how we just cleared the air, I don't want to do that."

His father smiled and then laughed. "Damn glad we cleared the air then."

"So am I. Oh, I'm going to bring Gen out for dinner tonight, if it is all right. I'd like you to meet her."

"I have met her, Son. Bring her out, though. I'll let Clara know." Senior's smile slid from his face. "This is your home. This is Hollister soil. Everything is yours. Everything. This ranch, that town, and all the bank accounts are yours. When you're ready to take the reins, I'm ready to hand them over."

"Could be a while." Andrew wasn't going to bullshit either of them. He couldn't function well without sleep, and until he could get the dreams under control, he couldn't move forward because, like Jeremiah said, he *was* stuck.

"Whenever you're ready." His dad repeated the words. "As long as it takes. I'll wait as long as it takes. Just knowing you're home for good is all I need."

Andrew broke off a bit of the biscuit and crumbled

it with his fingers before he looked up. "I love you, Dad."

"Oh shit. Now we're going to have to hug, aren't we?" His father rolled his eyes.

"Yeah, probably." Andrew stood up at the same time as his dad. They met at the side of the desk. The clasp was hard, and tight, and probably too long, but damn it, it felt good. When his father pulled back, the man rubbed the back of his neck. "I better get out to the barn and see what's going on."

"I'll be out shortly," Andrew said to his father's back. Senior lifted an arm in acknowledgement. Andrew smiled and picked up his coffee cup. Theirs wasn't a perfect relationship, but it was light years better than it had been yesterday. He looked up. "Yeah, Jose, I know. I know. You told me so." His father had been waiting for him to make the approach and clear the air. He glanced heavenward again. "Stop laughing."

CHAPTER 19

"Did you hear the Marshall Ranch house blew up?" The words were out of Edna Michaelson's mouth before she made it to the corner booth. All three of her cronies started talking at once. Gen glanced at Doc Macy and Ken Zorn, who were both eating breakfast.

Ken snorted and then choked. Doc Macy gave him a huge whack on the back. Ken almost faceplanted in his plate. He lifted an arm to prevent another slap from the vet. "Damn it, Noah, I'm not a cow, go easy."

"Wimp. You're not choking anymore, are you?" Noah Macy winked at Gen, and she laughed.

"What happened at the Marshall Ranch?" Gen asked and refilled Ken's cup, wiping up the coffee that had spilled when Doc Macy thumped him on the back.

"Propane tank exploded. Everyone's okay, just took

out a chunk of the ranch house. They are going to live in a big, fancy RV until everything is fixed. They have the Olsen crew contracted to come out and rebuild for them."

"The Olsens did my renovation." She glanced around her diner. "They were good, did the work on time and under budget. Which, in the world of construction, is amazing."

"Steve Olsen could squeeze a penny out of a stone," Doc Macy chuckled. "Trent has the company now for the most part, though. Steve is staying in the office and letting his son do the work. Heard only good things from the ranchers that they've worked with."

The women in the corner all gasped. Gen looked over to the booth at the same time as Ken and Doc Macy. Edna scooted out of the booth and double-timed it over to where Ken was sitting. "Did you get any reports of something weird happening at the Marshall Ranch?"

Ken put his biscuit down and slowly chewed it while staring at Edna. When he swallowed, he shook his head. "No, why?"

"Their house exploded."

"Because of a propane tank issue." He nodded.

"What if it wasn't propane? What if it was an attack?"

Ken Zorn leaned back in his chair and crossed his arms. "An attack. From whom?"

"Aliens." Edna nodded her head and looked back at

the women in the corner booth. One of the workers from the stockyard in one of the booths spit his coffee out and his friend covered his mouth, trying not to laugh. Edna turned and gave them the stink eye. "Don't you make fun of something you know nothing about."

Tegan Wells, the manager of the stockyards, dipped his head and tried desperately not to smile. "Apologies, ma'am."

Edna lifted her nose in the air and humphed a noise. She then turned her gaze on Ken. "Well?"

Ken sucked his teeth and then shook his head. "Ah, well, no. We didn't get any calls. Sorry."

"It's possible, though." Edna pushed him.

"That aliens blew a hole in Frank Marshall's home?" Ken asked, and Gen had to give him credit, he didn't laugh in the woman's face. The hands from the stockyard weren't so successful. Tegan cleared his throat and tried to get them to stop, but it was a losing battle.

"Yes." Edna nodded again and sent a wicked sidelong glance at the contingent from the stockyard.

Ken scratched his cheek. "Well, Edna, since we breathe air we can't see, walk on the earth due to a gravitational pull that we can't feel, and hear sounds through invisible waves that reach our ears, I'd say anything is possible."

"Yes, exactly as I thought. Gen, honey, we'll need more coffee, and bring me a caramel roll, please." Edna turned and almost jogged back to the table.

Gen turned her back on the corner booth and stared at Ken. "You shouldn't encourage her."

"Where in the hell did she get that idea?" Doc Macy asked, whispering behind his coffee cup.

"Allison." Gen rolled her eyes and Doc Macy laughed.

Gen retrieved a carafe of coffee and took Edna her caramel roll. The diner booths were full, and she made the rounds, making sure everyone had what they needed. She was just turning to go back to the counter when she watched a black BMW drive up and park in front of the diner. The door opened, and a tall blonde stepped out of the car. Gen chuckled. "She's not dressed for this area." A dark red pencil skirt, white silk blouse, and heels at least four inches tall completed the ensemble. Beautiful, to be sure, but not a local.

Both Ken and Doc Macy turned around. Ken swore low under his breath.

Gen looked back at the woman who was walking toward the door. "What? Who is that?"

"Mercy sakes! Look who showed up," Edna said loudly from the corner booth. "Stephanie Howard. How are you?" The woman smiled and walked over to the booth. She sat down and started visiting.

"She's a rattlesnake, Gen. Watch out," Ken warned when she grabbed a cup and saucer to take over to the table.

"I'll be fine." Drew's ex wasn't a threat to her. Drew had explained his relationship with the woman.

She approached the table and all the women stopped talking like an on-off switch had been thrown. Gen smiled and lifted the cup and carafe. "Hi, coffee?"

The blonde slid her eyes up and down Gen. "No. Thank you."

"No problem. Let me know if there is anything I can do for you."

Gen turned around and made it back behind the counter before the woman spoke. "Oh, there is something you could do for me. Tell Andrew his fiancée is back in town, please."

The entire diner went so quiet she could hear the heater on the coffee urn kick in. She drew a deep breath. And *that* was a line that shouldn't have been crossed. Ever. Gen put down the coffee cup and turned around. She crossed her arms and stared at the exquisitely made-up woman. "You are his ex-fiancée, Stephanie. Drew told me all about you. I could spread stories out of school, but I'm not that desperate to cause drama. Now, you can be nice and visit with your friends, or you can leave." She pointed to the sign above the passthrough stating her right to deny service to anyone. "I don't have to serve you, and I won't tolerate you trying to cause drama where there is none. So, behave yourself or go away."

Her customers in the diner were absolutely silent until Doc Macy started a slow clap. She looked over at him, and Ken started clapping, too. All of the stockyard workers in the first booth by the door took up the clap, and so did the next table.

Stephanie stood up and walked over to Gen. The clapping stopped and Stephanie smiled slowly. "You'll do." The woman stuck out her hand and, in shock, Gen took it. "Andrew is a good guy. Treat him well." The woman walked out and got back into her car.

Gen blinked and looked at Ken Zorn. The man shook his head, obviously bewildered, too. His surprised words followed the woman's exit. "People can change, I guess."

Gen shrugged and went back to work. If she didn't make a thing out of it, maybe no one else would either.

But news traveled fast, and gossip faster. Her phone rang two hours later while she was prepping for lunch service. She looked at the caller ID and smiled. *Drew.* "Hey, do you miss me already?"

"I do, but I just heard the strangest thing. Stephanie came for a visit?"

Gen laughed. "How in the world did you find out about that?"

"I told you, these men are worse than the old hens that Edna Michaelson sits with. Dusty, one of our hands, was picking up a maverick we bought from the stockyards and one of the guys there filled him in. Aliens and Stephanie. You've had an interesting day," Drew chuckled but then became serious. "She didn't cause a scene, did she?"

"No, if anything, I caused the scene." She snorted and then laughed.

"Excuse me?"

"Well, I basically told her she wasn't a threat, she was your ex, and that I didn't want or need drama. She could leave if she was looking for it. She walked over, stuck out her hand, said I'll do, and then left. She also said you were a great guy and to take care of you. I kind of liked her, and she's *really* pretty."

Drew made a strangled sound in his throat before he added, "Pretty on the outside, and that is interestingly weird that you think you like her."

"Right? What did your dad say when you told him I was coming out?"

"That was another interestingly weird conversation," Drew chuckled. "We cleared the air on several topics. He's happy to have you out. Things are better between us."

"Good." Her relief for their new understanding was immediate. The strained relationship between her and her mother was something she wouldn't wish on anyone.

"I'll be a little late picking you up. We're busy and we had a damn cottonwood limb fall on a fence, which, of course, means we need to make sure all the cows in that pasture are moved back."

"I can drive out. It wouldn't be any problem." She'd been by the turn off for the Flying H countless times.

"Are you sure?"

"Drew, I can drive. No problem. Just be at the house when I get there. It would be really awkward to show up and you are not there." She rolled her eyes. That would be her luck.

"Promise. I'll let you get back to work. I just wanted to make sure you were okay." His voice lowered into a rumble that echoed through her body.

She glanced around the kitchen as her face heated from the thoughts that flashed through her mind. "No, I'm fine. I'll see you at six?"

"Perfect. I can show you around before dinner."

"I'd like that." She sighed. "You're good for my soul, Andrew Hollister."

"I'm nothing special."

"To me, you are."

"And that's one of the reasons I love you."

The smile that split her face was one bolstered by pure joy. "I will never get tired of hearing that. I love you, too. See you at six."

She set the phone down when he disconnected and hugged herself. Was she actually floating six inches off the ground? She laughed and had to think for a minute what she was doing before the call. "Veggies," she said out loud although she was alone. One of the reasons she had a huge garden was to reduce the cost of her meals for the population. Jeremiah always tilled the plot she rented from Phil Granger, another resident who actually owned the land he'd settled on. Phil and Sara would have free reign to harvest whatever they wanted, which was usually only enough to feed their family of four. The acres of veggies she grew had become a side-hustle after harvest. Her restaurant meals, canning, and freezing weren't enough to utilize the crops that grew, so she sold the veggies from the diner, too.

Gen lost herself in prep and lunch service. There was a steady stream of customers and the takeout orders were up this week, but she had plenty of frozen dinners. Next week, she'd take inventory and rotate the stock to keep it fresh. She wiped down the counters and ran the mental checklist for the morning's work. She was done.

Gen locked the back doors and trotted up her stairs. She stopped about two-thirds of the way up. "What are you doing here?" The well-manicured man she'd known wasn't the same person she was looking at. His hair wasn't styled, his clothes were wrinkled, and his shoes were scuffed and dirty. "What happened to you?"

Avery pointed to his jaw. "Fuck you." The words were articulated so she could understand him, but obviously, his jaw was still wired shut.

She leaned against the rail of the stairs. "You can't blame me. That's what you get for being stupid, Avery."

Avery glared at her, his blue eyes full of hate. "You caused this."

"No, that was definitely *you*." She crossed her arms over her chest as he lifted out of one of the two small chairs she had on her small porch. "Do your parents know you're back here? Do I need to call my dad again?"

"Threatening me?" Avery stepped down a stair, staring at her.

"No. I want you gone, out of my life. Permanently." She'd do whatever it took to make that happen. Short of putting out a hit because really, did anyone do that?

"Funny, that seems to be our common ground." He took two more steps toward her.

A niggle of trepidation cautioned her, and she backed down a stair. She took out her cell phone and pushed the profile picture for Jeremiah. "I'm calling my brother. He's across the street. You'd be well-served to be gone before he gets here."

Remi growled, "Gen, I'm waiting for a patient."

"Avery is here."

Without hesitation, Remi replied, "I'm on my way."

She held out the phone toward Avery. "He's coming. You better get out of here and stay away from me."

Avery continued down the stairs until he stood on the same step as she had. "Common ground." He narrowed his eyes at her, trotted down the rest of the stairs, and tucked around the corner between her diner and the hardware store.

Jeremiah appeared seconds later. "Where is that fucker?"

Gen pointed, and Jeremiah took out after him. She plopped down on the stairs and clenched her hands together. Avery looked like shit. He'd lost a huge amount of weight. His spray tan was gone, his skin a pasty white color. The dark circles under his eyes made the crazy way he was looking at her even more bizarre.

"I can't find him. Are you sure it was him?" Jeremiah jogged back to her.

"Oh yeah. It was him. He was waiting at the top of the stairs for me. I wasn't going to play games, so I called you."

"Is your apartment locked?"

She nodded. "I've locked it since the first time he showed up. God, Remi, why in the hell is he back here?"

Jeremiah sat down on the step below her. "I don't know, but I can find out. I'll call Dad tonight when he's home. Are you okay? He didn't touch you, did he?"

"No, he didn't touch me, and I'm fine, just confused. He looked like he'd been through hell." Gen pulled her scrunchie out of her hair and let it drop to her shoulders.

Jeremiah shook his head and stared at the little walk between the buildings. "I don't know where he went. That's weird. A guy in a suit isn't hard to see in this little place."

"He wasn't wearing a suit. Khakis and a grey polo." She rubbed her forehead. "I don't care where he went as long as he's gone. I told him that I wanted him out of my life permanently, and he said that's what he wanted, too. But if that's what he really wants, why show up here?"

Jeremiah turned around slowly. "What did you say?"

Gen repeated herself. "Why?"

"Just spitballing here, but I think he may have dipped over the edge. He wants you out of his life permanently."

"Yeah." Gen nodded and rubbed her eyes. She was tired and she still had to drive to the Flying H—and meet Drew's father as 'the girlfriend.'

"Gen, he might have meant 'permanently' differently than you did."

Jeremiah's tone made her blink her eyes to get him into focus. "What do you mean?"

"Permanently gone as in dead."

She snorted. "I told myself I'd stop short of putting out a hit on him to get him out of my life."

"Would he?" Jeremiah lobbed the question at her.

Her mouth dropped open. "Avery? Kill me? No." She shook her head and then stopped. The way Avery had looked at her... She dropped her eyes to her brother, and Jeremiah lifted an eyebrow at her. She sighed, "Well, thanks for that." She shivered, sitting in the sunshine. Would Avery actually... She closed her eyes. No, but then again, who would have thought the man would have taken a baseball bat after her and Andrew?

"I'm not saying he meant it that way, but be careful. Lock that door behind you, and keep the kitchen door to the diner locked, too."

"I'm careful, but I'll pay extra attention. I need to go

get ready. I'm heading out to Drew's for dinner tonight. I'm meeting his dad."

Jeremiah stood and offered her a hand up. She took it and let him help her up. "Hope that goes well for you. You know it is just a formality, right? The man is crazy about you."

"No more than I am about him. I do know it is a formality, but it still makes me nervous."

"You'll be fine, and you need to tell Drew what happened here." Jeremiah waved at the stairs.

"I will when I see him tonight. He's not going to be happy."

"Who could blame him? Just be careful. I've got a bad feeling about Avery, and my gut is rarely wrong." Jeremiah stared at her.

"I will be extra-cautious. I trust your instincts." He was always right about people, and she wasn't going to test his judgement.

"Good. Call Drew when you leave for the ranch so he'll know you're coming."

"I will. Thanks for playing the white knight." She gave him a quick hug. "You should go back to your patient."

"I have a few minutes. I'll be in my office for an hour, after that I'm going to go lock up and head home. If you need me, you know how to reach me. Take care."

"I do, thanks again. Night." She waved at him and headed up the stairs. She opened the screen door and unlocked her apartment. She stepped through the door and immediately threw the deadbolt. After living here for all this time, locking the doors seemed foreign and frightening. Strange what you come to value. Avery had shattered her sense of safety in her perfect little community.

CHAPTER 20

Andrew glanced at his watch. He wasn't going to get a shower before Gen came out. He tickled Jasper's ribs, moving him into a trot, and Dusty did the same to his mount. They were missing two cows and they were both ready to deliver anytime. Damn things had gotten out when the branch had dropped the fence, and from what they could tell, had wandered toward the highway. The fence line would hold them, but they needed to be closer to the barn in case they needed help delivering.

His phone rang and he grabbed it, answering it without looking at the face, his eyes continuing to scan the horizon for the damn cows. "Hello?"

"Hey, I'm leaving the diner heading your way." Gen's voice washed over him. He slowed Jasper to a walk.

"I'm not at the house." He shot a look over at Dusty. "I can meet you at the turn-off and ride to the house with you." He lifted his eyebrows at Dusty in question.

The man nodded. "I can tie him to my saddle and wrangle the damn cows. No problem."

"Are you sure?" She sounded worried.

"I am. Don't be nervous. Senior won't bite." If he did, Andrew and he would have words again.

"No, I'm not."

He pulled his mount to a stop and pointed to the hill almost to the road. The damn cows. Where in the hell they were going, he had no idea. He and Dusty turned their horses and followed after them. "You don't sound too sure of that."

"I'm… Drew, I'm sure I'm being paranoid because of what Avery said and then what Jeremiah said, but I think I'm being followed."

"Hold up, Avery?"

"Yeah, he was on my porch today. Jeremiah thinks he may have threatened me."

"Tell me exactly what happened." He glanced toward the road and then back to where Hollister laid.

Gen explained the events. "And now there is this silver SUV behind me."

"Where are you?"

"Just passed the turn off for the Reeber place." She chuckled, but he could tell she was worried. "I'm being stupid, right?"

"Just cautious. You're about five miles away. Speed up a bit and see if they keep up with you."

"Okay." She was silent for a moment. "No, they sped up."

"Can you see who is in the SUV? One or two people?"

"It looks like one, but the sun is on the windshield. I don't know."

"Is it a full-size SUV?"

"No, one of those crossovers."

"Okay, Gen, I'm sure there is nothing going on, but I want you to slow down. See if they pass you." He leaned over Jasper's head. The horse needed no further encouragement.

"Shit!"

He saw Dusty's horse in his peripheral vision, matching speed with his mount. "What?"

"Drew!" He heard Gen's shout.

"What's happening?"

"He rammed me. Oh, God!"

"Are you still on the road?"

"Yes! I floored it."

"Fly, baby, I'll be at the turn off." He nudged his spurs into Jasper's side and the horse flat-out ran over the scrub brush.

"There." Dusty pointed toward the road. Gen's truck flew over the hill with the smaller vehicle right on her ass.

"Gen, you'll need to slow down, or you won't make the turn." He shouted the words into the phone.

It seemed to happen in freeze frames. Gen's truck slowed; the silver vehicle rammed her. Her truck fishtailed. The rear tire of the truck gouged the side of the road, and she flipped back onto the road, catching the silver vehicle's rear quarter panel. Gen's truck rolled side-over-side. The smaller SUV spun and end-over-ended, stopping about a half-mile from where Gen's truck landed.

"Fence!" Dusty screamed at him.

He pulled back on Jasper's reins, aiming for the fencepost so the horse would see the object. They launched over the ornamental wood slats of the fence that showcased the Flying H's turn-off. The horse clambered and scrambled up the embankment to the highway. His horse's shoes clattered on the pavement as he raced to Gen's truck. Drew was out of the saddle and down on the ground, crawling into the cab of the vehicle before the dust kicked up by the rollover had settled. His heart slammed against his chest as terror gripped him. He couldn't fucking lose her, too. He punched the airbags out of the way. "Gen!"

"Drew. Drew, thank God. I'm okay. I think." She hissed and held her head. "I can't get down. Help."

"I'm here, babe." His hands shook like fucking leaves in a windstorm as he reached for her. He moved her hair that was draping to the ground. Blood dropped from her scalp, but her eyes were clear.

"Thank you, Jesus," he said automatically. He pushed on the airbag, moving it out of the way. "Put your arms up. I'll try to catch you, but you need to brace for a fall."

"Okay." She stretched her arms out, and he pulled his knife from his pocket, flicked it open, and sawed through the nylon strap at her shoulder. It released, and he worked on the lap belt, holding her as best as he could in the awkward position. When the belt snapped free, she fell on top of him. "Damn it."

"What's hurting?"

"My shoulder. Where the seatbelt held me."

He righted her as gently as he could. "I need to get you out of here. I can smell gas." He could hear something hissing in the engine compartment. Fire was another immediate concern. He helped her out of the upside-down vehicle, and once she was free, picked her up, carrying her to the side of the road.

"I called Doc and Ken Zorn," Dusty yelled as he ran from where he'd left his horse on the other side of the fence line.

Drew put Gen down. "No, don't sit up. Lay right there." He ran his hands down her legs and her arms.

"I think I'm okay. I bumped my head pretty hard, and my shoulder is hurting. What happened to the other driver?"

Andrew looked down the road. Like he gave a shit what happened to the bastard that had rammed her. "I don't know."

KRIS MICHAELS

Gen put a hand on his as he examined her. "Drew. Go find out if they are okay."

Dusty stood up. "I'll go."

Andrew shook his head. "No." He was going to meet the fucker that had done this up close and personal. "You stay with her. Doc should be here shortly." He could hear the wail of Ken Zorn's siren. The deputy was miles away. He glanced down at Gen one more time.

"I'm just shaken up. I'll be okay. Go." She patted his hand.

He nodded and stood. As he jogged over to where Jasper was ground-tied, he felt the drape of his past settle on his shoulders. Deadly intent focused him like nothing else could. The son of a bitch in that vehicle had tried to kill Gen. Drew mounted, and he and Jasper moved toward the silver SUV which had settled on its top. He took the rifle from its boot on his rig and kept it pointed at the hunk of metal. He dismounted and walked to the front of the vehicle.

Bending down, he stared into the confines of the smashed SUV. The windshield was pushed out from the inside. Deflated airbags hung like used balloons. There was a small amount of blood, but no body. He stood and lifted his gaze, sweeping around for... *There.*

He once again mounted Jasper and shoved the rifle into its boot. He unfastened his lariat and tickled Jasper's ribs. The horse's lope ate up the ground. Andrew snarled, lifted his rope, and started circling the

256

loop in the air. It had been a hell of a long time since he'd done any roping, but the slow-moving target ahead of him might as well be standing still. The man turned around, saw him, and almost fell. *Fucker*. He righted himself and ran faster. As if he could outrun a fucking stallion. Drew waited until Jasper was almost on the asshole and tossed the rope around the man and dallied the rope around the saddle horn. He pulled Jasper to a stop. The horse damn near sat down he stopped so fast. The rope tightened, and the man jerked down at the other end, flopping onto the ground. Drew kept tension on the rope and moved Jasper forward.

"Let me go! Keep that animal away from me!" Avery shouted, his words slurred as he rolled, trying to get out of the rope that was tight around his chest. Jasper danced, his hooves within a few feet of the man on the ground but not near enough to cause damage. Although, that was a thought. He'd seen men shredded by hooves because they weren't paying attention. Drew kept the tension tight on his reins while he held his internal debate. Killing wasn't new to him. He'd killed for his country. *Hooves or rifle. Both?* The fucker would be just as dead. Although, if Jasper killed the miserable son of a bitch on the ground, they'd label the horse a killer. Ken Zorn's vehicle screamed over the hill as Drew reached for his rifle. He backed Jasper up and the fucker who'd just gotten to his feet fell again.

"Andrew. Don't do what you're thinking about.

Seriously, don't put your hands on him. I don't want to do the paperwork." Ken's concerned voice over his vehicle's PA carried to where he sat, debating that very thing.

Andrew stared at Avery. The fuckwad turned his head to see the sheriff's car and then looked up at him.

Then he did it.

The bastard went and smiled at him as if he'd won. *Not fucking likely.*

Drew turned Jasper toward the highway and tickled his ribs. "Wait! Stop!" Avery yelled from the ground behind him. "You're dragging me!"

Andrew kept moving forward, and he aimed straight for every clump of brush he could find. Avery screamed obscenities the entire half-mile back to the road. Drew stopped Jasper in front of Ken Zorn and loosened his lariat, snapping it from Avery's body.

Ken walked around Drew's horse and put his hands on his hips. "Well, I'll give you credit. You didn't put your hands on him."

Andrew stared at Avery. Hundreds of small cuts littered his face, chest, and arms. Like Drew gave a flying fuck. He looped the length of rope and put his lariat around his saddle horn. Gathering himself in the time it took to stow the rope, he spoke in measured tones when all he wanted to do was rage against the stupid fucker that kept making Gen's life a living hell. He leaned on his saddle horn and spoke directly to Ken Zorn. "I witnessed the entire thing. He rammed his vehicle into Gen's. He tried to kill her. Dusty witnessed it, too."

Ken shook his head. "Stupid city slicker, do you not yet understand not to fuck with people who are tougher than you'll ever be?"

Avery groaned and rolled onto his back. Zeke's truck skidded to a stop on the road, pulling Andrew's attention from the waste of sperm on the ground. A plume of dust rose across the highway as his father's truck flew down the access road from the ranch, too. Drew got off his horse and walked him back to where Gen was. Senior's truck slammed to a stop on the other side of the road, and his father was out of the vehicle in a heartbeat.

"I'm okay." Her words were out of her mouth before he could ask. "Was it Avery?"

"Yes." He ground out the word.

Gen sighed. "When will he be out of my life? I don't know what I need to do to make him stay away."

Senior strode down the incline as she spoke. "I know what to do, and I have the money to make it happen. Don't like to flaunt it, but damn it, this is the last straw. You rest assured you won't have any more problems from that waste of breath." He glanced at Andrew. "You two don't ever need to worry about him again. That bug is going to be squashed."

"Thank you." He stared hard at his dad, hoping to convey how much he meant the words.

His father nodded and headed over to where Ken was handcuffing Avery, who was still on the ground.

Drew knelt beside Gen as Zeke examined her. A small flashlight flicked from eye to eye. He had her grip his hand, push and pull, and moved to her legs, doing basically the same thing. "Neck sore?"

Gen nodded. "A bit. Yeah, but muscle-sore, not I-broke-my-neck-sore."

Zeke laughed as he worked. "You'd know the difference?"

Gen snorted. "I'd like to think so, but probably not." He watched as the doctor palpated her abdomen. "I think you're going to be fine, but I'd like to get you into the office and x-ray that shoulder."

"Drew, take my truck. I'll ride Jasper back home and brush him down." His father tossed him his keys.

He caught them in mid-air. "Thank you."

"Just hope he doesn't try to throw me. My bones don't bend much anymore." His father picked up the reins, and Jasper rubbed his head against his father's chest. Not much chance of that happening. The horse was feisty, but not ill-mannered.

"Hey, Doc, can you check him out just to make sure he won't expire on the way to jail?" Ken pointed to where Avery sat on the ground.

Zeke may have muttered a cuss word or two, which grew Drew's respect for the doctor. "Take her into town to the clinic. I'll be there shortly." Zeke grabbed his bag and walked over to Avery.

"Did the glass from his windshield cut him like that?" Gen asked after he helped her up. She leaned into him, and he held her gently.

"Yeah, let's go with that," Andrew deadpanned.

She lifted her head and winced. "Ouch. I think I'm going to need a hot shower and a couple painkillers."

"I'll make sure you get whatever you need. Come on." He helped her up the embankment.

"I'll be back for your statement after I book this guy," Ken called after them. Andrew lifted a hand in acknowledgement.

"Jeremiah's gut was right again," Gen said once she got into the truck. "That man knows crazy."

Andrew glanced at her and put his hand on her thigh. "I never want to live through anything like that again. I thought I'd lost you."

Gen placed her hand on his. "I'm still here."

Drew squeezed her leg gently and drove like an old man back to town. He pulled up at the clinic, turned off the truck, and unfastened his seatbelt.

"I'm sorry."

"For what?"

"A crazy ex?" She shrugged and winced. "Ouch, boy howdy, remind me not to do that again."

"Your ex has issues, but once Senior sets his mind to something, it is done. He won't be a problem any longer." And if Avery showed up again, Drew would ensure the bastard was gone. There were a lot of wide-open spaces in South Dakota and Wyoming. "How sore are you?" He pushed her hair back and examined the cut at her hairline. "That might need stitches." The blood had caked but the cut still wept a bit.

"I'm hurting but so grateful. He could have killed me and himself." She shivered and crossed her arms, hugging herself.

"He didn't, and he won't be able to do anything from jail. If I know Senior, he's calling every person he knows to make sure that asshole gets the maximum sentence for each of his crimes. People out here don't take to strangers making problems."

She nodded. "Guess I made one heck of an impression tonight," she chuckled. "Do you think the truck's totaled?"

He nodded. "Oh yeah. The fact that you're not hurt worse is a miracle." He leaned over and kissed her. "I'll have the hands pull it out of the ditch with a tractor and either pull it to the ranch or load it on a trailer and take it there."

"Thank you." Gen closed her eyes. "I don't think I'm going to open tomorrow. I need to put a note on the door."

"I'll take care of that. I'd like to take you out to the ranch tonight. You won't have to climb stairs and you can take it easy. Clara would love to fuss over you, and if you're there, I can stop in and check on you."

"Wouldn't that be awkward?" She blinked at him. "Unless we're in separate rooms."

Andrew huffed. "That would be the day. We're

adults, Gen. If Senior or Clara have a problem with our sleeping arrangements, they can suck it up." He cupped her cheek in his palm.

"Then I'd love to have someone take care of me tonight." She leaned into his hand. "I'm afraid when all this settles in, I'll have a freak-out."

"I'll be with you all night." He kissed her temple. "Longer if you'll have me."

She looked up and winced. "What?"

"I know what I want. I want you."

"It's way too early to talk about this. Isn't it?" She blinked up at him. Her eyes were wide, but he caught the wistful look of hope there.

"It isn't. Not for me. I know where this is ending for us. I don't need a church wedding, but if you want one, we'll have it here. Invite the town." He ran his thumb carefully over a bruise that was darkening on her chin.

"When?"

"January." He'd take her to a tropical island for their honeymoon.

"The diner is slow then. Corrie should be up to speed... that's actually workable." She lifted her eyes to his. "Are we engaged?"

He nodded, holding her gaze. "Unofficially. I want to do right by you. Buy you a ring, ask your dad for his permission, take you out to dinner, and ask you properly."

"Then unofficially, I accept. Officially, I'll wait for that moment." She moved to let him kiss her when there was a knock on the window. Drew lifted his eyes. Zeke pointed to the clinic. Drew didn't even acknowledge the man. Instead, he lowered for that promised kiss. He was taking this moment and every spectacular, wonderful moment a future with his woman would provide. Damn the rest of the world.

EPILOGUE

Zeke Johnson rolled his shoulders, cracking his back and neck before he picked up his beer. The music was low tonight as were the lights inside The Bit and Spur. A hell of a night. Gen's ex was batshit crazy. Not necessarily his medical diagnosis, but it was his honest belief the guy was off his rocker. Thankfully, he didn't deal with ailments of the mind. He didn't know how Jeremiah did it. The man worked with the Guardians that transitioned through the Marshall Ranch. They were his primary patients and his bread and butter.

Zeke had worked with Doctor Cassidy a couple of times, but after the event at the Marshall Ranch a couple weeks ago, he was now a card-carrying Guardian employee. On standby. He chuffed a laugh and took a drink of his beer. He'd signed more papers than a library could hold and knew enough to never say a word about anything he'd seen at the ranch. Which had been... horrid. Death was everywhere. He sure as hell wouldn't say a word.

He took another sip of his beer. He should be at his small house, working on the addition he was building, but after the mad dash to the Flying H turn-off tonight and the x-ray he'd done on Gen, a cold beer sounded more enticing.

"Hey, Doc." Tegan Wells leaned on the bar beside him.

"Tegan. How are you feeling?"

"Good. Thanks for stitching up my hand this morning. I can't believe I sliced it that deep."

Tegan held up his bandaged hand and wiggled his fingers.

"Lucky you didn't go any deeper." As it was, the cut was something he needed to monitor, deep and prone to opening due to its location. "You come and see me in the morning, I want to make sure it isn't getting infected or you haven't pulled my fancy stitch work out."

"I'll be there. Need to offload a trailer of mustangs we have coming in first thing, so probably about nine."

"I'll be there. If I'm not, I'll leave a note as to when I'll be back."

"You ever think of hiring someone to do appointments and such?" Tegan accepted a beer from Declan and handed him a five.

"The county has suggested it. But the pay is next to

nothing." He'd have to supplement the salary with his income. With Jeremiah in the office most days, they were getting by.

"I'll text you before I leave. I'm running two men down as it is, so knowing you're there would be better."

"That works. You have my number."

"I do. Night, Doc."

"Night."

Tegan ambled back to the booth where he and another man were sitting. Zeke rolled his shoulders again. He should head home. He was tired and hungry. Zeke glanced at the door when it opened. He did a double-take and his jaw damn near hit the bar.

A tall, sexy blonde walked in. Her honey-colored hair fell in a halo of curls around her shoulders. The tight, red skirt she was wearing showed off a toned body and long, long legs. She was beautiful, without a doubt. She was probably someone's girl or wife. Although, he didn't see a ring on her finger.

Declan flipped the bar top open and hugged her. "Did you get unpacked?" Zeke cocked his head. Score one for girlfriend. He lifted his glass and examined the bubbles before he took a sip.

"I did. Be a sweetheart, would you? I need a glass of Chardonnay."

"Coming right up." Declan hustled behind the bar and poured a glass for her. The woman took it and glanced around the bar. Their eyes met and Zeke nodded. She smiled and continued her inspection of the interior of the bar.

"Declan, you need to redo these booths. They're ratty."

"I haven't had any complaints," Declan grunted. "What are you going to do with yourself now that you're back?"

Zeke blinked and glanced over at the duo. That didn't sound like a relationship question.

"Try to start over." The blonde shrugged. "See if this town will forgive and forget."

Declan gave a snort. "Excuse me, have you lost your mind? Hollister isn't forgiving, and reputations are hard to live down."

The blonde took a sip and nodded. "Well, I don't give a shit what they think of me. I know who I am now, and I've worked hard to become the person I am."

The door opened, and two couples came into the bar. Their talking made it impossible for Zeke to hear the rest of the conversation. Not that it mattered. Whoever the woman was, he wished her well. Hollister was a good little town, its citizens solid. If she'd changed like she'd claimed, the people would bend. But only if the change was real. Most would wait it out before they made a call.

He finished his beer and tossed down a five onto the bar. "See you later, Declan."

"Hey, Doc, have you met my sister, Stephanie?"

Zeke stopped and smiled. So, definitely not girl-friend, then. "I haven't. Ezekiel Johnson."

"Is Doc a nickname or a profession?" Stephanie extended her hand.

He took it and held her hand in his. He wasn't going to lie, her soft hand felt damn nice in his. "Profession."

"Oh, people or animals?" She smiled, and he was mesmerized. She was beautiful.

"People. Sometimes they act like animals, but most definitely people." He let go of her hand.

"Well, it's nice to meet you, Ezekiel."

"Zeke," he corrected her.

"Zeke," she amended. "I hope to see you around."

"I'm sure you will." He gave Declan a nod and headed out the door. The night had suddenly taken a turn for the better. *Stephanie Howard.* He made his way to his truck. He didn't know Declan had a sister. He turned the ignition and looked back at the bar. What reputation did she have? How had she changed? He shook his head. It really wasn't his business, was it?

With a last glance to the bar door, he put his truck into gear and headed home.

To read Zeke's story, click here!

To read Frank's story, click here!

To read Valkyrie's story, click here!

ALSO BY KRIS MICHAELS

Kings of the Guardian Series

Jacob: Kings of the Guardian Book 1

Joseph: Kings of the Guardian Book 2

Adam: Kings of the Guardian Book 3

Jason: Kings of the Guardian Book 4

Jared: Kings of the Guardian Book 5

Jasmine: Kings of the Guardian Book 6

Chief: The Kings of Guardian Book 7

Jewell: Kings of the Guardian Book 8

Jade: Kings of the Guardian Book 9

Justin: Kings of the Guardian Book 10

Christmas with the Kings

Drake: Kings of the Guardian Book 11

Dixon: Kings of the Guardian Book 12

Passages: The Kings of Guardian Book 13

Promises: The Kings of Guardian Book 14

The Siege: Book One, The Kings of Guardian Book 15

The Siege: Book Two, The Kings of Guardian Book 16

A Backwater Blessing: A Kings of Guardian Crossover
Novella

Montana Guardian: A Kings of Guardian Novella

Guardian Defenders Series

Gabriel

Maliki

John

Jeremiah

Guardian Security Shadow World

Anubis (Guardian Shadow World Book 1)

Asp (Guardian Shadow World Book 2)

Lycos (Guardian Shadow World Book 3)

Thanatos (Guardian Shadow World Book 4)

Tempest (Guardian Shadow World Book 5)

Smoke (Guardian Shadow World Book 6)

Reaper (Guardian Shadow World Book 7)

Phoenix (Guardian Shadow World Book 8)

Hope City

Hope City - Brock

HOPE CITY - Brody- Book 3

Hope City - Ryker - Book 5

Hope City - Killian - Book 8

Hope City - Blayze - Book 10

The Long Road Home

Season One:

My Heart's Home

Season Two:

Searching for Home

STAND ALONE NOVELS

SEAL Forever - Silver SEALs

A Heart's Desire - Stand Alone

Hot SEAL, Single Malt (SEALs in Paradise)

Hot SEAL, Savannah Nights (SEALs in Paradise)

Hot SEAL, Silent Knight (SEALs in Paradise)

ABOUT THE AUTHOR

Wall Street Journal and USA Today Bestselling Author, Kris Michaels is the alter ego of a happily married wife and mother. She writes romance, usually with characters from military and law enforcement backgrounds.

Made in United States
North Haven, CT
22 January 2023

31435713R00154